Moonbeams *and* Ashes

Tales of Mystery, Love, and the Paranormal

MARGARITE STEVER

"Clean Heist" was published in the 2021 edition of The Crowder Quill.

"Gold Grand Prix" was published in Writers Digest Show Us Your Shorts Collection in 2014 and Maine Review in 2015. Light editing has been done to improve the flow.

"One Foggy Night" was published in the 2017 issue of The Crowder Quill. Slight edits have been done.

"Lost Sheep" was first published in Anthology 2019 Sleuths' Ink Mystery Writers.

Publishing Coordinator – Sharon Kizziah-Holmes
Cover Design – Sharon Kizziah-Holmes

Paperback-Press
an imprint of A & S Publishing
A & S Holmes, Inc.

ISBN -13: 978-1-951772-98-7

DEDICATION

This book is dedicated to my cousin, David Hughlett, who battles leukemia like a mighty warrior. I never see him without a smile and a little joke to make others laugh, no matter his own pain and fatigue. He is an inspiration who tells me that I am his favorite author.

This one is for you, David.

ACKNOWLEDGMENTS

I'd like to thank the many people in my life who've shown me encouragement and support throughout my writing journey.

Thank you to my husband who tolerates my nesting habit when I'm absorbed in my work and doesn't complain too much about hectic writing-related activities; my mom who is so proud of my work she keeps my publications displayed on her coffee table and a binder of every rough draft I've ever sent her; my sister who kept after me to join the Joplin Writers' Guild until I finally did and found it to be one of the best decisions I ever made; my family who listens when I gush about a particular publication or upcoming event; my critique partners past and present: Bonnie Tesh, April Brock, Darrell Lacey, Summer Farnsworth, and Claudia Errington who always offer insightful comments and never withhold the truth if something needs work; my writers' groups: Joplin Writers' Guild, Sleuths' Ink Mystery Writers, Ozarks Romance Authors, Ozarks Writers League, and Missouri Writers Guild; and my dear friends who patiently listen to me go on and on about my stories, often reading them to make sure they're not drivel.

Special thanks to Priscilla Purcell Brown, who planted the seeds of this book in my mind several years ago; Terry McDermid who has always been generous with her time and wisdom; and my two dearest friends, Tammy Walker and Lori Divine, who are there for me no matter what.

You all made me believe in myself and my work. I couldn't have done it without you.

Clean Heist

Monica pushed her buggy down the aisle of the big box store and searched for canned goods on the sparsely stocked shelves. The pandemic had gone to people's heads, and there was hardly any food left at the store. She sighed as she reached for the last can of green beans, still there because it was hidden behind the hominy.

She studied her nearly empty buggy. Unable to find toilet paper, paper towels, or hand sanitizer, she'd be forced to make another stop. She smiled at the generic laundry soap she'd scored. A few weeks ago, she wouldn't have even noticed it. Things had changed, and she was grateful to have snagged the bottle from the almost empty aisle.

After paying for her meager purchases, she drove to the next store. She was about to open the door of her minivan when a news story on the radio caught her attention. Someone had been breaking into tractor trailers and stealing supplies. Another truck had been hit the night before, and authorities were looking for a blond, white male in his thirties driving a blue Chevy minivan. No license plate number was available.

Hair standing up on the back of her neck, she started her vehicle and drove home. She frowned at an unfamiliar old Honda parked in the street in front of her house. She looked around, but didn't see anyone. Careful to be as quiet as possible, she took her groceries inside.

Voices carried through the floor vents from downstairs, drawing her attention. "I can't let you have it for less than fifty, dude. This is choice product right here." He laughed before continuing. "I guarantee you won't find this high-quality product anywhere else right now."

Suspicion darkening her thoughts, Monica crept down the stairs to the game room and peered around the corner. Her boyfriend, Greg, stood with a man in rumpled sweatpants and an air of desperation in front of a huge stack of boxes. She squinted, trying to read the markings from her vantage point.

She felt dizzy as the letters became clear. The largest cache of Purell Hand Sanitizer she'd ever seen was taking up nearly half of her basement game room. Shaking her head to clear it, she marched into the room.

"Greg, who's your friend?" She leveled her best glare at the man she loved.

"Monica." He looked around, focusing on anything but her face. "I didn't know you were home."

"Obviously." She crossed her arms and narrowed her eyes further.

Their nervous guest cleared his throat. "Listen, I don't need any trouble. I have five kids. I can't find this stuff anywhere. I need it, man. Have you ever tried to keep a toddler's hands clean?"

Greg straightened his shoulders. "Fifty dollars a case. Take it or leave it."

Before Monica could say a word, the man

thrust a wad of cash into her boyfriend's hand and dashed out the basement door to the back yard, clutching a case of Purell.

Greg slid the money into his pocket and turned to her. "I'm doing business here. You're always bugging me to get a job and help with bills. Well, this is my part-time job."

"Where did you get all this hand sanitizer? And why?"

He avoided her gaze. "It's a business opportunity. That's all."

"Where did you get the money to pay for it?" She studied him. "You did pay for it, right?" When he didn't respond, she pressed. "Please tell me you didn't steal a bunch of Purell."

He laughed long and loud, his eyes wide with a crazed gleam. "It was a clean heist. I saw a Target truck in the lot with nobody in it. The trailer lock wasn't very good. It opened easy. I had to hurry, so I only swiped the good stuff. It didn't take any time at all to load it in the van. I was gone before anybody even knew I was there."

"You did *what*?" She clenched her fists to keep from throttling him.

"Babe, Target's insured. They won't be

out anything. I saw an opportunity to make some money and took it. You should be proud."

She shook her head, trembling in fury. "You stole something that people desperately need from a truck heading to a store where people buy supplies. You think I should be proud? You used my minivan? My house? Oh, no. This stops now."

She fished her cell phone from her back pocket and dialed the police. Greg shoved her to the floor and ran outside as the dispatcher answered.

"I've found the guy stealing stuff from big trucks. I have a whole bunch of the stolen property in my house. You should send someone over before he comes back." Choking back a sob, she told them where she lived and to have the officer come to the basement door.

Minutes later, a firm knock sounded and Monica opened the door to two police officers.

"Good afternoon. I'm Officer Black, and this is Officer Sutton. I understand you have something you'd like to show us."

Wiping a tear from her face, she pointed to the Purell. "My boyfriend just told me he stole this stuff from a Target truck last night. It's probably not his first time, either. He used my van to do it, too."

Officer Black took her statement while his partner searched the house. His radio crackled, and they heard Officer Sutton announce he'd located the suspect hiding in a closet and taken him into custody.

"It looks like he snuck back into the house and was waiting for us to leave. Good thing we got here when we did." Officer Black flipped his notebook closed and slid it into his shirt pocket with his pen. "My partner has Greg secured in the car. He'll stay there with him. We'll send someone to collect the Purell soon. It's evidence."

She nodded, feeling hollow inside.

"Do you plan to continue to allow him to reside here?"

"No," she whispered. "I can't trust him."

"You should change your locks as soon as possible." He patted her shoulder. "Calling us took courage. It was the right thing to do. Try to take comfort in that."

Nodding, she walked him to the door and locked it behind him.

Staring at the boxes of stolen goods, she asked the universe, "Why in the world didn't he steal toilet paper instead? Risking jail time for that makes much more sense."

AUNT ROSE'S CABIN

My hand-drawn paper map indicated I should, "Veer left onto hidden driveway by ancient stump." I eased my old Chevy Impala up the mountain road with no idea how I was supposed to recognize an ancient stump or a hidden driveway. With no GPS signal, I had to rely on what I was given.

I bounced down the rutted lane until I spotted an old mushroom-covered stump. Drawing even with it, I turned down the trail that could be considered a driveway and crept along until I came to a log cabin. The morning sun reflected off the windows and solar panels making the cabin feel welcoming. Parking by the front porch, I took in the view of the surrounding mountains.

Aunt Rose had no children and never married. She'd left all of her siblings, nieces, and nephews something in her will when she passed away several months ago. Her three siblings, including my father, had received equal shares of her large house in the city. My cousins all received one personal item. She left me the beautiful rosebud bracelet I wore. She'd noted in her will that I'd enjoy it because of my artist's soul.

I thought everything was settled, so I was shocked when a different lawyer contacted me last week. Aunt Rose had a separate will for this cabin that no one had ever mentioned.

"Rose instructed me to give you this when you arrived to collect the cabin keys. Whatever's inside that envelope was important to her and is for your eyes only." The attorney smiled and patted my shoulder as he handed me the large brown envelope along with the paper map.

Something so personal shouldn't be opened in the law office, so I'd slid it into my bag and told him I'd open it when I reached the cabin.

Breathing deeply, I clambered out of my car, looked up at the sky, and asked the universe, "Why would Aunt Rose keep this place a secret?"

Clutching the keys, I lumbered up the front porch steps. After slipping the key into the lock, I swung the door open with a only slight push. Aunt Rose had decorated this place, all right. A green velvet couch faced the large native stone fireplace. A blue leather recliner sat to the right of the couch at an angle. Facing the recliner on the other side of the couch was a mauve wingback chair.

I wandered into the modern kitchen and found a round oak table with four matching chairs. Upon the table, an open journal with a blue pen nestled in the crease drew my interest. It should prove to be interesting reading later.

Walking into the bedroom, I discovered a cedar bedroom set and thick blue carpet on the floor. Down the hallway, the den was cozy with a large oak desk, built-in bookshelves, and beautiful paintings on the walls. From the bathroom that was small and had a little window for natural light, I made my way back to the kitchen and sat down at the table.

I withdrew the envelope from my bag, tracing my finger over my name written in Aunt Rose's flowery script. Feeling the breath rush from my body in a heavy sigh, I opened it. My eyes burned with unshed tears as I read the letter.

My Dearest Jillie,

If you're reading this, I've been gone for a while. There's a lot about me that no one knew. None of the rest of the family cared, but you always asked me questions about my life. You wanted to know where I worked and what I did there. You asked about my hobbies, interests, and if I had a boyfriend. You inquired about my health. You wrote to me often.

Do you remember what you did at age three when you found out I lived by myself? You gave me your favorite doll, Becky, so I wouldn't be lonely. You'll find Becky in the living room curio cabinet. That gesture told me more about the person you'd become than anything else you ever did.

You bucked family tradition and pursued an education in the arts. You refused to bend to their expectations. You stayed true to yourself.

Those are the reasons I chose you to inherit my secrets. The cabin I've left you was my special place. I hope it will be the same for you. You are about to learn more about me than you could ever imagine. I lied to you. I'm sorry for that. I was never the person you thought you knew.

You'll receive a visit from a man named David Buchanan soon. He's the only person you can trust. He'll explain everything, but you must tell no one. You have something important that you must give to him. You'll know where to find it when the time is right.

You may be approached by someone from an organization called Gryphon Group. These people are dangerous. Don't go anywhere with them. Don't trust them. The cabin should be a safe place. If they find it, call David immediately and tell him you need an extraction. He knows what it means. You'll find his cell phone number in these papers.

I've enclosed maps to safe locations and phone numbers of people who are willing to help if you're ever in trouble. Feel free to read my journals. They'll tell you everything you wanted to know about me. The cabin and everything in it are now yours.

I love you now and forever. I will be with you in spirit as you discover who your old aunt really was. My legacy is now yours, Jillie. Guard it well.

Love,
Auntie Rose

I buried my face in my hands and sobbed. I was just calming down when I heard a sharp knock at the door. Creeping across the room, I peeked through a sidelight. On the porch stood tall dark headed man wearing blue jeans and a red flannel shirt. His brown eyes were somber as he studied the door.

"Who is it?"

"My name's David Buchanan. Rose asked me to come and talk to you."

I opened the door and offered my hand, which he shook gently. "I'm Jill Carlson," I said, my voice sounding like sandpaper drawn across the bark of an oak tree.

"It's nice to finally meet you. Your aunt spoke highly of you." He stared at me for a moment and shook his head. "Forgive me. You favor her so much with your fair skin, dark hair, and eyes so deep brown they're nearly black. Seeing you is like looking at a younger Rose."

Tears filled my eyes again, so I stepped aside to give myself a moment. "Would you like to come in?"

He nodded. "Thank you. We have much to discuss."

I led him into the kitchen and looked around in dismay. "I'd offer you something to drink, but I didn't bring anything. I'm sure everything in the fridge is spoiled by now."

He smiled. "Actually, I stocked the essentials for you. Rose gave me a key in the event of her demise with instructions to keep the place up until you arrived." He withdrew the key from his pocket and placed it on the table. "I imagine you want that now that you're here."

I walked over to the fridge to check out our choices. Finding bottles of water, I grabbed two. I handed him one, then opened and sipped the other as I reclaimed the seat across from him. "You said we have things to discuss."

David nodded. "Have you had a chance to read Rose's journals?"

"No. I just arrived and read the letter she left with the lawyer. She said I was to trust you and to run the other way if anyone from Gryphon Group contacts me. What in the world could an accountant like Aunt Rose have gotten mixed up in to cause her so much paranoia?"

David's gaze bored into mine. "Rose wasn't an accountant. That was her cover. She was an undercover operative for Gryphon Group, a top-secret government agency."

I laughed. "You're telling me Aunt Rose was a spy? You've got to be kidding. She was an accountant. She traveled to corporate locations performing audits, not espionage."

"You said she told you to trust me, right?"

"Yes, but this is ridiculous!"

David stood. "I think I know what will help. Come with me. I need to show you something."

I acquiesced and followed him. He walked into the den and turned a print of Van Gogh's *The Starry Night* slightly to the right. A wide panel slid open to reveal a secret room.

I couldn't believe my eyes. The room was filled with weapons of all descriptions. Everything from hand guns to futuristic-looking devices filled several built-in racks.

"No." I shook my head. "These can't be Aunt Rose's. Why would she need these?"

David leaned down so we were eye to eye. "Jill, she was a spy. I was her partner. If I hadn't been called away on another assignment, she'd still be alive."

After regarding him for a moment, I spoke. "She told me to trust you. The letter was in her handwriting, so I'm going to give you the benefit of the doubt. Please continue."

He pointed to the phone on a shelf. "That's a satellite phone. You can call from anywhere with that. No cell towers required." He gestured to the rest of the room. "Should you ever have a need, all of these weapons are fully functional and the ammo for each one can be found in the drawers beneath the gun racks. This was Rose's personal collection. Nobody knows you have them. I suggest you keep it that way."

I looked around. "I know how to use the hand guns and rifles, but not these other things."

"I'll be happy to show you sometime."

"Thank you. What else do we need to discuss?" I asked.

"Let's go back into the living room." He righted the painting and the panel slid closed. "The windows all have a special coating on them so you can see out, but no one can see in."

"That's handy." I shook my head in wonder.

"When someone turns onto the driveway, a little red dot appears on all of the windows. You should also hear a soft ping. You may not have heard it today because you're overwhelmed."

Plopping into the recliner, I covered my eyes with my hands. "You could say that. I'm assuming Aunt Rose believed I'd be in danger from this Gryphon Group. If they're part of our government, why would they want to hurt me?"

"The agency has been corrupted. The leadership is involved with some big-time criminals. Rose was collecting evidence against them. They killed her. They wouldn't hesitate to kill you, too."

"Why? I don't know anything." I stood and paced.

"They may never bother you, but I promised Rose I'd make sure you were prepared." He stood and clutched my shoulders. "This is serious. I haven't been able to find the micro SD card where she documented the evidence. You won't be safe until we find it."

"I don't understand why she chose me. I'm not a cloak and dagger kind of girl."

"Rose trusted you to carry out her last mission, but she wanted you to have this place, so you could finish writing that book you told her so much about."

"She told you about my book?" I sniffled, my eyes stinging with sudden tears.

"Yeah, she talked about you a lot."

Tears slid down my cheeks. "Aunt Rose was amazing. Tell me how I can help."

"We need to find the micro SD card. That will enable me to take the monsters down."

"Those things are tiny. It could be anywhere. I'll look for it, but all of her personal belongings were distributed amongst the family."

"She told me that you'd find it. She told me to have you search your artist's soul."

"My artist's soul . . ." I looked at my bracelet.

I slipped it off and examined it with great care. The wires making the stem were woven in an intricate pattern. The bud was made of pieces of hammered metal. On a hunch, I grasped the delicate rosebud and twisted. It unscrewed with little effort. Once the pieces were separated, a small object fell out of the hollow.

"I think I found the micro SD card." I grasped it with trembling hands.

"Yes! Now we can put those murdering monsters behind bars where they belong." He wrapped me in a bear hug. "Rose was right to choose you."

"Thanks, but it can't be that easy. Can it?" I asked.

Whatever he was about to say was cut off by the soft ping, accompanied by a red dot on every window.

"One of us must've been followed. Come on, we need to get to the weapons room." David seized my arm and pulled me along. He grabbed Aunt Rose's journal and letter while I clutched my purse and key.

"Do you know who it is?" I asked. "Maybe someone is lost."

"Not likely. One of us probably picked up a tracking device in town." He tilted the Van Gogh and we stepped into the room.

"What are we going to do?" I whimpered.

He handed me a duffle bag from a nearby

hook. "Grab whatever you know how to use and the ammo that goes with it. We don't have much time. The micro SD card won't do us any good if we die before we can do anything with it."

I filled my bag and followed him out of the room. He righted the Van Gogh and led me to the bedroom closet. He pulled me inside and closed the door. Once the door was shut, the back wall opened into a secret passage. We ducked through the opening and David closed the panel.

We didn't speak as we hurried through the tunnel. We emerged in a garage with several nondescript vehicles and a few sports cars. I couldn't help running my fingers over a gorgeous cherry red Camaro. I'd always wanted a car like this.

"The Camaro is another part of your inheritance, but I recommend you leave that one here for now. It doesn't exactly blend in."

I followed him to a black SUV and climbed into the passenger seat. "Sure. Where am I going?"

"You're coming with me to a secure location. Don't worry, I'll keep you safe." He sped out of the garage and onto the road.

I thought maybe we'd given the bad guys the slip, but then I saw a brown van coming up behind us fast. Glancing at the speedometer, I knew we were in trouble.

"They're behind us! What do we do?" I could feel the panic sliding into my belly.

"Keep your head down and pray for now," he said as he pushed the accelerator to the floor.

I slid down in the seat as far as I could and closed my eyes. I'd nearly convinced myself we'd outrun them when I heard gun shots and the unmistakable sound of glass shattering.

I risked a peek behind me, sickened by the ragged remains of our back glass. "Tell me this car has a backward facing gun."

"Nope. Return fire while I try to shake them." He spun the wheel to the right, taking us off the road and into the woods.

I took a handgun from my bag and loaded it with shaking fingers. Aiming at the car behind us, I pulled the trigger. My shot hit their windshield, obstructing the driver's vision. He lost control and slammed into a tree.

"That was close," David mumbled.

Terror seized me. "Do you think I killed

them? Oh, tell me I didn't kill them!"

Glancing over at me, his eyes softened. "No. You didn't kill anybody. That was a reinforced government vehicle. It's little crunched, but I assure you everyone inside is just fine. With luck, they'll be in prison soon."

He left the woods and turned onto a dirt road, little more than a cow path. We drove for several miles on various Missouri back roads until I was so lost I knew I'd never find my way home. He finally left the last dirt road and turned onto a barely discernable grass trail. Bouncing along the uneven ground, we were both lost in our thoughts.

He pulled into the barn behind an old dilapidated farmhouse surrounded by old growth trees. "We'll stay here until it's safe."

"Is this one of the places on the list Aunt Rose gave me?"

"Yeah. It's my favorite because it's so difficult to find. Don't worry, it's fully stocked with provisions. We can stay here for quite a while."

Once settled into the farmhouse, David led me to a hidden office where he examined the evidence Aunt Rose had died to protect. "This goes all the way to the top. Even the director's been doling out bribes to cartels."

"It's hard to believe our own government people are betraying our country like that." I felt my shoulders droop under the weight of all I'd learned.

He paused in his perusal of the documents and gazed up at me. "We aren't all bad, Jill. There are still patriots working to keep everyone safe. Good people like Rose was. Like I am. Thanks to Rose's sacrifice and smart thinking in giving the evidence to you, the scumbags in these reports are going to be locked up for a long time."

Contacting the appropriate authorities to turn over the information, David made a secret copy in case of the unexpected. A few days later, Gryphon Group was shut down pending an investigation.

I went back to Aunt Rose's cabin and read her journals. My aunt led an incredible life, which inspired me to move into her cabin and write an entirely different book. The story is about an amazing spy named Rose who spent her life saving the world, while her family believed she was nothing more than an accountant.

GOLD GRAND PRIX

The full moon showing through the deep purple clouds appeared ominous against the night sky as Jasmine hurried home. Icy wind pierced her thin sweater rendering it virtually useless. Her high heels clicked eerily on the sidewalk as she increased her pace. Glancing furtively around, she could swear she saw a pair of glowing eyes watching her from the bushes. Hearing a rustling sound, she quickened her steps again.

She should have known this evening was doomed from the very beginning. Feeling pressured into an ill-fated date with her mother's neighbor, Jasmine really tried to connect with Bill. Unfortunately, the man never ceased his incessant chatter. His idea of an interesting topic revolved around his fishing boat, golf stats, or successful career as the city's premier dentist. He was so full of himself that she wasn't even certain he realized that she hadn't gotten into the car with him when he left the restaurant.

Jasmine had reached her limit with Bill and stomped away in a huff. Now she was rethinking her decision to walk home rather than call someone to come and get her. She just couldn't suffer through any more of Bill's obnoxious conversation. If she ever saw him again, it would be far too soon.

She was kicking herself for accidentally leaving her cell phone at home. There were six blocks left to her apartment and her feet were already so blistered that she doubted her shoes would come off without prying them off with a butter knife. Her frozen toes would probably be permanently shaped like the pointy toes of shoes that were great for sitting, but not meant for walking.

The rustling became louder and seemed to be following her. Was that a growl? She looked over her shoulder toward the line of hedges and saw glowing eyes that were gaining on her fast. She broke into an awkward high-heeled run, making it half a block before she twisted her ankle and crashed to the frozen sidewalk in a frightened heap.

The growls were getting louder and the glowing eyes were almost to her. Just as she was certain she was about to die, she heard a car come to a stop on the road beside her. The driver made a loud noise, and when Jasmine looked back toward the bushes the eyes were gone.

"Didn't anyone ever tell you that it isn't safe to go out by yourself late at night?" the clean-cut middle-aged driver asked.

She looked at the driver as he spoke and felt an odd sense of familiarity with him. She was certain she must know him from somewhere. She was about to ask if they had met when he stepped from the car and offered her his hand to assist her to her feet. Whimpering as she regained her feet, she nearly stumbled into her rescuer.

"Thank you," Jasmine said still feeling that strange sense of connection. "Do I know you?" she asked.

"I believe we met once long ago. You can call me Ed, and you are Jaz."

Taken aback by the use of her childhood nickname Jasmine smiled weakly. "No one has called me that in a very long time. I go by Jasmine now."

"Yes. Well Jasmine, let me give you a ride home. I can't stand the thought of you hobbling the rest of the way when you can barely stand."

Never, in her entire life, had she accepted a ride from a stranger. However, Ed wasn't really a stranger. He said they'd met a long time ago. She knew in her heart that was true. He seemed so nice, and she had the strangest urge to hug him. Nodding her acceptance, she let Ed help her to the passenger side of the vehicle.

She was about to climb inside the warm car when she noticed it was identical to the one her grandmother had when Jasmine was a little girl. She'd always loved the car, but she hadn't seen it since she was a small child.

"It's rare to see a 1970 Grand Prix in gold these days," she whispered. "My grandmother had one just like this when I was a little girl. She said it always made her sad to drive it because it was my grandpa's pride and joy. He passed away when I was a baby."

Jasmine couldn't believe she had just blurted out something so personal to a virtual stranger. She'd never been this chatty before. It must be all the stress of the evening that had her spilling her childhood history.

"I'm sure she missed him very much," Ed whispered.

He put the car in gear as soon as Jasmine was settled on the tan vinyl seat. She was oddly soothed by the vibration of the big motor. New cars just didn't have the same feel and sound as the classics. The fuzzy dice swayed beneath the rear-view mirror with the motion of the car. She felt safe and happy for some odd reason that she couldn't quite explain. They arrived at her apartment building far too soon, and she stifled a sigh of disappointment.

She turned to her rescuer. "Thank you for the ride, Ed. I really appreciate it."

"My pleasure. And Jasmine? Don't walk around by yourself at night. You had a really big and dangerous looking dog stalking you. He could have ripped you apart. I think he smelled your leftovers."

She'd forgotten all about her leftover

chicken in the take-home container from dinner. She had stuffed it down into her oversized handbag and promptly forgotten all about it.

"How did you know about my chicken? Come to think of it, how did you know where I live?" She felt the tingle of fear kiss the back of her neck.

Ed gave her a serene smile. "Jaz, I know many things about you. Think of me as part of the family. Now I must be going. Can you make it inside all right?"

"Yes, I think so," she replied, feeling an odd sense of love fill her heart.

Inside her little apartment, she pried her shoes off with a butter knife as planned. She was soaking her aching feet in a bucket of cool water when she felt the uncanny urge to call her grandma. Glancing at her watch, she decided midnight was way too late to be calling. She promised herself that she'd go visit her grandma the next morning. That decided, she soaked her feet for a while and tottered off to prepare for bed. She was so tired that she was only mildly annoyed to discover she'd lost one of her favorite earrings. The large silver hoops with dangling hearts had been a gift from her mother for her 21st birthday. After the night she had, she was certain to never see it again.

Her grandma was excited to see her the next morning. They drank tea and chatted about mundane things for a few minutes before her grandma asked about her date the night before. Jasmine told her about the horrible meal with Bill, the frigid walk most of the way home, her lost earring, and her odd rescue from a hungry dog and a twisted ankle.

"The man seemed really familiar. He said we'd met a long time ago. You should have seen his car, Grandma. It was just like the Grand Prix you used to have. It was even the same color. Now that I think about it, it even had the same kind of fuzzy dice on the mirror."

"It's funny you say that about the car. I still have it. It's out in the barn under a tarp. I actually dreamed that I heard it start up last night. It was an odd dream. That car hasn't run in at least twenty years." Her grandma's eyes misted a little with her words.

"Do you mind if I go look at it, Grandma? I would really like to see it again," Jasmine asked.

"Let's both go look at it. I haven't seen it in years." The elderly woman grabbed a thick, wool coat from the entryway closet.

The temperature was chilly, but not unpleasant as they made their way out to the barn. It took both of them to open the door, as no one had used it in several years and it was quite stuck. After a great deal of effort, the door finally opened to reveal the dusty interior of the old barn. Jasmine's grandpa had once cared for his farm animals and stored his hay in the building, but now it was full of old boxes and broken furniture.

Stepping inside, they picked their way over to the far corner where the Grand Prix sat beneath a tarp and at least two inches of dust. Her grandma slowly slid the tarp off the car, her eyes filling with tears as she beheld her late husband's prized possession.

Jasmine decided to give her grandma a little privacy to compose herself and opened the passenger door. She caught her breath at what she saw. There, on the passenger seat, was a large silver hoop earring with dangling silver hearts – the one she had lost the night before.

A Bigfoot's Big Dreams

"Quick! Hide! Here come humans!" Harry tugged on Sassy's arm.

"Don't you think it's time we let them know that we share the planet with them?" She jerked her arm from his grasp.

"Sassy Sasquatch, I'm surprised at you!" Harry clasped her arm again and tugged with more insistence.

"You do remember that they once worshipped us as gods, right? I've heard that life was really good back then. The humans brought us their best food and baubles. We lived in huge temples, and our word was law."

"Sh! Here they come." Harry pulled her

down behind a boulder with him.

Two female humans crashed down the path toward them. Dressed in clothes that barely covered their bodies, they continued past the boulder without a single glance in Harry and Sassy's direction.

Once they were out of sight, Sassy stood. "I don't know why they even bother wearing anything at all if they aren't going to protect their legs against the brambles. Human logic still eludes me."

Shaking her head, she ambled toward the river, leaving Harry to do as he pleased. He caught up to her and grabbed her shoulder making her look up to his superior nine-foot height.

"Don't you remember what we learned at Bigfoot High School? The humans turned on our ancestors and hunted them for food. They ate us! Do you seriously think we should give them the chance to make steak out of us again? We nearly went extinct!"

Shoulders slumped, she heaved a deep sigh. "No, I haven't forgotten. Our scarcity is why I'm with you. I'm the only female for 500 miles, and you're the prince of the region. So, we're stuck with each other whether we like it or not. We're expected to make little baby Bigfoots to perpetuate our species. I think the humans owe us for that."

Harry roared in irritation. In answer, Sassy picked up a fallen tree branch and hit a giant oak with all her strength. They repeated the process several times.

"Darn it, Sassy! Sasquatch is the most respected family name on this continent. Any Bigfoot would be thrilled to be a part of our tribe, but you don't care. You make it sound like we hate each other, too." He crossed his arms over his massive chest.

"Well, we certainly don't like each other, Harry. We have nothing in common. I want to go out and explore. To learn new things. I would love to learn to operate those machines that the humans roll around in. They go really fast, and it looks like fun. Even the ones on two wheels look interesting. All you want to do is stay in the cave and breed."

"We are supposed to stay in the cave and breed. My father would be furious if he discovered we were out during the day. It's easier to hide in the dark."

"I don't want to hide anymore!" Sassy shouted.

Harry took a deep breath and let it out

slowly. "If you reveal yourself to them, they will lock you in a cage. Don't you remember when they tried to capture Uncle Biggs? He barely escaped. His territory is still infested with human Bigfoot hunters. He had to relocate to a higher elevation."

She felt the righteous passion leave her as she turned back toward the cave. "You are right, my prince. Let's go home. I feel like a nap." She walked beside him back toward their cave in silence.

Sassy's sadness weighed on Harry's conscience. He'd upset her. She was the most precious jewel of his people, and he had snuffed the fire from her eyes.

"Wait, Sassy. I have an idea." He gestured toward the east. "There are old human ruins not far from here. I bet if we go there, we can find some baubles for you."

She shook her head. "I don't want baubles. I want freedom."

He couldn't think of anything else to say as he watched his mate enter their cave and walk all the way to their nest in the back. She hugged her knees to her chest and soon fell into a fitful sleep.

As afternoon turned to evening, she slept on. Harry was overcome by the urge to do something special for her. Under the cover of darkness, he snuck into the nearest human town. He crept along with great stealth. A few dogs noticed him and barked, but the people ignored them and didn't bother to investigate.

He shook his head and muttered, "Humans have lost all of their animal instincts."

He searched around for a while before he found what he sought. Sneaking behind the dwelling, he was careful to keep to the shadows. Leaning up against the side of the house was a green two-wheeled machine that he had seen humans ride along the mountain trails. Without a sound, he grasped the handlebars and pushed it back to the cave.

Sassy was peeling apples with her obsidian knife when he returned. She gazed up with shadows beneath her eyes. "What do you have there?"

"It's one of those riding contraptions the humans use. It's not the big kind that goes really fast, but I thought you might like it. I bet it will be fun once you learn to ride," he said, ducking his head.

"You brought me human wheels? Harry,

that's so thoughtful!"

"Well, I thought about what you said. I can't give you the freedom you desire, but I can give you this small joy. I've seen the humans ride these things, and it doesn't look too difficult. I heard one of them refer to it as a bike."

That night Sassy and Harry took turns learning to ride the green bike. It didn't take long before they were riding up and down the mountain trail. They rode until the sun was peeking over the horizon. Sassy laughed with unabashed joy, feeling the first stirrings of true love for her mate. She watched him dash down the trail, the rising sun behind him turning his fur into a golden halo. He'd never attempted to have fun with her before. Perhaps Prince Harry Sasquatch wasn't such a bad Bigfoot after all.

They pushed their bike into the cave and curled up together to sleep the day away, content in their budding love for each other. Harry drifted off, his thoughts on the idea that perhaps they had a chance for those baby Bigfoots after all.

SILVER'S CURSE

———◇———◇———◇———

My best friend's party was depressing. I hadn't dated since my break-up with my last mistake, and I wasn't in the mood to watch other couples be happy together. I finished my champagne and headed to the coat closet for my jacket. I was glad that I only had one glass of champagne and was able to drive myself home. It was way too cold to walk.

"April, you aren't leaving yet, are you?" Tina called as she rushed up to me.

"It's a wonderful party. I'm just not feeling very social."

"I understand, but I hate for you to go so early."

I hugged her. "Thank you for having me. You throw an amazing party."

Tina laughed. "I'm so happy you decided to come. Drive safe, and get some rest. Things will get better soon."

I lumbered to my car, which was parked up a slight hill from Tina's house. My heels scraped against the cold pavement as I trudged along. I really needed to get on with my life.

A rustling in the brush near my car startled me. I turned toward the noise to find a pair of glowing eyes staring at me. I hurried to my car and started the engine. As I was backing out of my spot, my headlights illuminated a large silver wolf in the brush. He stood perfectly still and never took his eyes off me.

Turning onto the street, I hurried home. I parked on my short gravel driveway and made my way to the house. I was just about to insert my key in the lock when someone grabbed me from behind, slamming my face into the rough wooden door.

"I told you that you couldn't get rid of me with some lame restraining order," the man I'd once thought I loved growled.

"Chad, let me go!" I demanded with more

confidence than I felt.

"No! You're mine! If you aren't mine, then you're dead!" he shouted in my ear. I tried to twist around to look at him, but I saw the moon reflecting off the knife he held instead.

Leaves crunched as something ran across the yard toward us, but I couldn't turn my head to see what it was. I heard a vicious snarl, and Chad was suddenly on the ground squealing like a pig.

I couldn't believe my eyes. The silver wolf from Tina's house had my abusive ex-boyfriend pinned to the ground with his knife-wielding fist firmly gripped between powerful jaws. The jerk's blood pooled on the frozen ground as he punched the wolf with this free hand.

Without wasting any time, I unlocked the house and grabbed the baseball bat I'd put inside the door after the break up. I ran toward the pair wrestling on the ground. The man who'd once broken my arm for turning off his football game looked up at me with murderous rage in his eyes. This was a battle of survivor and it was either him or me. I swung my bat, hitting him in the shoulder as hard as I could. The wolf let go, and Chad grabbed for me. I swung the bat again, hitting him in the leg this time.

He started to rise, but my canine hero stood in front of me with his hackles raised and snarled. The wolf was quite a sight with blood dripping from his muzzle.

"You hit me! You stupid whore!" Chad shouted

"You came here to kill me!" I shouted back. "And you've hit me plenty of times."

Whatever he might have said in return was cut off by a police car pulling into the driveway with lights flashing. My wolf protector ran into the woods behind my house as the police officer approached.

"What's going on here?" the officer demanded.

"Chad and I used to date." I paused to squelch the hitch in my voice. "We split up a few months ago, and he's been stalking me ever since. I have a restraining order against him. He attacked me when I got home tonight." I swallowed the sob building in my throat. "He had a knife and said he was going to kill me."

"I'm not saying anything," he told the officer. "I know my rights."

After a few more minutes of

interrogation, the officer arrested Chad and explained that one of my neighbors had seen him attack and called the police.

Back inside the warmth and safety of my modest home, I locked myself in and leaned back against the door. The terror of what might have been slammed into me with the force of a freight train. Chad would have killed me if that wolf hadn't stopped him.

I kicked off my heels and was walking to my bedroom when I heard a crash outside my kitchen door. Tiptoeing across the floor, I peeked out through the window. The silver wolf sat on my patio next to an overturned flowerpot with his back to the house. He looked as if he was standing guard, which touched my heart, making me feel a little safer. He'd saved my life. He was more than welcome to stay.

The next morning as I walked to my car, my rescuer approached me. He accompanied me, watching me get into my car. In my rearview mirror, I saw him sitting by the driveway as I drove away to go to work. He was there when I returned that night. This became our daily ritual.

I decided to call him Silver and put a bowl of water, some food, and an old comforter out on the patio for him. I was surprised that he stayed every night as the temperatures hovered around freezing for days at a time. The weather became more dangerous as time passed, and the local meteorologist was calling for significant ice accumulation.

Snug and warm in my house while reading a book, I heard the sleet begin. With wood stacked in my fireplace and more beside the hearth in case of power failure, I was all set. But, I wondered if Silver was still on my patio. That old comforter would be no protection against this sleet. Peeking outside, I found him huddled next to the house. I couldn't leave him out there. Could never live with myself if I let him freeze to death.

The logical part of my brain told me not to let a wild animal into my home, even as my hand turned the knob and eased the door open a few inches. I couldn't leave him out in the ice. He'd become more of a companion to me than a wild animal over the past several weeks.

When I opened the door wider, Silver moved to stand in front of me. He cocked his head to the right and stared at me with those big blue eyes.

"Come on in. It's too cold for you to stay out there."

He let out a small whine as if confused. I stood aside, and in my best coaxing voice said, "Come on, boy. It's nice and warm in here with me."

Silver took a hesitant step forward and stopped. I beckoned him with my hands and whistled softly. He took a few cautious steps into my home and looked up at me when I closed the door. His fur was encrusted with ice, and thinking how cold he must be was breaking my heart.

"Come on, Sweet Silver." I walked into the living room, hoping he'd follow. "I'll find a nice soft blanket for you."

I rummaged through the linen closet and found an oversized plush throw. Spreading it in front of the fireplace, I sat down beside it.

"Come on, my sweet wolf. We need to warm you up," I crooned.

He approached me with a look of uncertainly. Once he decided I wouldn't hurt him, he lay down on the blanket next to me. With great care, I drew the blanket edges around him and ran my fingers through the soft fur of his head. To my surprise, he leaned into me. I put one arm around him and held him until he stopped shaking.

Leaving him snuggled in his throw, I grabbed dinner from the kitchen. The small roast in the Crockpot had cooked nice and tender. I scooped two bowls full of pot roast, potatoes, and carrots. I put an ice cube in one bowl to cool it down for Silver so he wouldn't burn his tongue. Back in the living room with the bowls of roast, I set one in front of my furry friend.

His eyes glowed as he lunged for the food. Curled up on the couch with my own dinner, I enjoyed the sight of this magnificent animal wolfing down my cooking. He didn't lift his head until his bowl was empty.

The power went out around 8:00 p.m., so I lit the fire I'd prepared. Silver snuggled on his blanket and fell asleep. I watched him for a while before my own eyes grew heavy, and I joined him in slumber.

The next morning, I awoke with the sun shining in my eyes through the living room window. Sitting up, I stretched my stiff muscles, and looked toward the fireplace for Silver. I smiled when I saw he was still sleeping.

What a beautiful animal, I thought, but then he began to twitch like he was having a seizure. My heart pounded as I jumped to his side. I wrapped my arms around him and tried to hold him still, not sure what else to do.

The twitching intensified, and his joints began popping. He panted hard and looked up at me with large terrified eyes. Licking my cheek once, he then leapt away from me. I started to follow him, but his warning growl stopped me.

I stared helplessly as he started to glow. Then I watched in horrified fascination. Silver, who had kept me company for several weeks, transformed into a tall muscular man with silver blond hair and cerulean blue eyes.

"What the hell?" I screamed and shrank back in shock. "How did you just do that?"

He looked down at himself in stunned silence. Then he laughed long and loud before speaking. "April, you broke my curse! Thank you!"

He watched me backing away and held his hand out to me in entreaty. "Please don't be afraid of me. I'll never hurt you."

"How exactly did you come into my

house as a wolf, eat as a wolf, and sleep as a wolf, but suddenly become a man?" I shrieked.

"Please stop backing away," he begged. "I will not harm you."

"Yeah, well," I began in a shaky voice, "you better start explaining things."

"My name is Nicholas, and I was cursed. I was a selfish, egotistical man. I did not treat women well. I used them for my own pleasure and didn't care what happened when I was finished. I took what I wanted and then left them used up and alone. One day I crossed a woman who had the power to stop me."

"Go on. I'm listening," I urged, inching closer.

"I had some fun with a woman named Maria. She thought we were in love. When she told me that she was carrying my child, I told her that she would have to deal with it on her own because I was not marrying some low-class trollop."

He took a deep breath before continuing. "Instead of crying as I expected, she called me a monster. She cursed me to roam the earth as a lone wolf until a woman showed me true kindness and compassion."

Nicholas looked at me and whispered, "You did that last night."

"How long have you been cursed?"

"One hundred and twenty-five years." His breath hitched. "Everyone I knew is gone. The world I knew is gone. My child is gone, and I never even met him or her. I never saw Maria again."

"So, you finally have your humanity back and nowhere to go?" Tears threatened to spill from my eyes.

"Please don't cry for me. You've given me a most precious gift. You have granted me my freedom. I can now spend the rest of my life atoning for my sins. And I would like to begin by ensuring your safety and happiness. I vow here and now that no one will ever break your bones again."

AUNT IDA

I looked around the old house where I was stuck until I sorted out Grandma's estate. My family had chosen to keep as much of the original Victorian décor as possible to keep Aunt Ida happy.

I never knew Aunt Ida. She died in 1899 when she fell down the stairs. The legend was that she couldn't bear to go to her reward while her three children were small.

She'd been seen in the nursery watching over babies of each generation to live in the house. Grandma's babies were last. None of the rest of the family wanted to move in.

Though she'd been seen hundreds of times, no one had ever heard her speak. I hoped she would understand me because I needed to warn her the house was going to be sold.

I climbed the stairs, hating the black and gray striped wallpaper. Floorboards creaked beneath the gray carpet as I made my way down the hall.

With a twist of the doorknob, I entered the old nursery, my heart racing. The room was decorated with blue striped wallpaper. Someone had loved stripes.

"Aunt Ida? I need to explain some things to you." I spoke softly so I wouldn't startle her. A cool breeze raised goose bumps on the back of my neck.

"What shall we discuss?"

I turned to find a transparent apparition wearing a conservative pale blue Victorian gown standing in front of the hallway window, her dark hair pulled to the top of her head in a tight bun.

"I'm your niece. Christy. My grandmother was your niece, Edith. Grandma recently passed away."

"I'm aware of Edith's passing, child. I was with her in her last moments and guided her to her reward."

Tears ran down my cheeks as I gazed into

her sad eyes. "What about your reward? You must be ready to cross over. You've stood guard for well over a century. We're selling the house, and you won't have any family to watch over."

Her shoulders slumped. "I won't leave my baby."

"Your babies grew up and had children of their own. They're all waiting for you in Heaven."

"All but one. My fourth child, who will forever be an infant."

"You only had three children."

She straightened to her full height, hovering a few inches above the floor. "No, my dear, I had four. Albert never had a chance to grow. His life was stolen."

I whispered, "What happened?"

"He was a month old. Hearty and hale. He had my eyes. One morning when I came into the nursery, I found him strangled with one of my hair ribbons." The pain in her voice was palpable.

I reached for her hand, watching as mine passed through it. "I'm sorry. I had no idea. That story wasn't passed down."

"I imagine not. Gregory was already in the room and whisked Albert from my arms screaming he wasn't his baby. I ran after him, reaching for my son. He slapped me, knocking me down the stairs. When I awakened, I was merely a phantom."

Her voice grew louder. "I heard him telling my other children they were not to speak of Albert ever again. He wasn't to be buried in the family cemetery because he wasn't his son. My husband didn't believe Albert was his because he looked like me! I know not where he put my son, but he's still in the house. I feel him."

I thought for a moment. "Could he be buried in the backyard?"

"He's within these walls. I hear his cries echoing in the night. I've searched but cannot find him."

"We'll find him. I'll see that he receives the burial he deserves."

"You would do that?"

"Of course. We're family. Let's make a list of the places you've looked." I glanced around for a pen and paper.

"I've searched everywhere but the basement. I cannot enter that space."

"There's a basement? No one ever mentioned it."

"I haven't seen anyone enter there since

Gregory last walked these floors."

Suspicion niggled the back of my mind. "Can you show me the entrance?"

She floated down the stairs to a wall in the kitchen that held several heavy shelves. "The door is here."

I cleaned off the shelves and examined the supports. "Can you tell me precisely where the door is?"

She went into the shelves and stood dead center of them, stretching her hand to the wall.

Grabbing tools from the kitchen drawer when Grandma had always kept them, I ripped the shelves down. I ran my hand around the space, feeling the outline of the door.

Slicing the wallpaper, I yanked it down revealing a door without a knob. A small piece of wood had been used to connect the door to the wall, keeping it from moving.

I wedged the claw of my hammer against the wood and swung the door open. I turned on my cell phone flashlight and stepped over the threshold.

Peering over my shoulder, I found Aunt Ida hovering just outside the doorway. "Can you come in now?"

"No. Something is still keeping me out. Please find my baby."

I hurried down the stairs. I'd just reached the floor when I heard the crying. Following the sound, I wound around old furniture and wooden crates. The cries were louder at the furthest crate from the stairs. Using my hammer to pry the lid open, I wasn't prepared for what I found.

I'd expected to find the skeletal remains of a baby. I was shocked to find the remains of a woman wearing a pale blue Victorian gown cradling the baby in her arms.

I snapped some pictures with my phone and called the police. While we were awaiting the authorities, I showed Aunt Ida the pictures. Tears flowed as she beheld her son, still wrapped in her arms.

"I remember now. I took Albert from Gregory before he slapped me. I never thought about what he did with my body. I worried only for my son. Thank you, Christy."

As I watched, Albert appeared in my dead aunt's arms briefly before they both vanished into the ether.

"Rest in peace now," I whispered.

DEVIL ROOSTER

I became acquainted with pure evil when I was five years old. He was so nice at first, all fluffy and cuddly. He fit in the palm of my hand and looked up at me with such innocence. I loved him as soon as I discovered him in my Easter basket. I knew he'd grow up, but I had no idea he would become the antithesis of cuddly. It didn't take long for him to show me his true nature.

He was about six months old the first time he attacked me. I was just learning to ride my bicycle, and our farm in the Ozark Mountains of Missouri had lots of space to accommodate a beginner such as me. My bike was a little too big for me, so I had to struggle just to get up on it.

I'd pushed my bike up the hill to the end of our gravel driveway because riding downhill was much easier for my tiny legs. Taking care to keep my balance, I mounted my bike with its high seat and took off down the hill doing my best to pedal with my short legs.

He came out of nowhere. I was enjoying the wind in my face one minute, and the rooster from hell was attacking my ankles and calves the next. He was all over me, his sharp beak like an ice pick, stabbing me over and over again.

I rode screaming down the hill, pedaling faster, but he was too quick. I swerved and circled, but I couldn't shake the devil rooster. His black and green feathers were all ruffled up, his hackles were fully raised, and his screeches probably woke the dead. I finally figured out that I could put my feet up on the handle bars where he couldn't reach them if I got up enough speed. I rode like that all the way to the house screaming and crying for Mom.

My mom ran out of the house armed with a wooden spoon. She yelled at the devil rooster and swung her spoon at him when he turned to attack her. She showed him who was boss, though. No one could best my mom in a wooden spoon fight. She wielded it with the utmost skill. The rooster finally relented and ran away from her expert spoon play.

Mom wiped my tears and hugged me tight. "Hush, my sweet girl. That mean old rooster can't get you now. Mama is here to protect you. Just don't tease him anymore, and he'll leave you alone."

She honestly thought it was over, but I knew better. I'd seen the look of pure hatred in that rooster's eyes. He wouldn't be happy until my legs were striped with gashes from his talons and spurs.

That night at dinner, I told Daddy what had happened. He shook his head and told me, "Beth, we need that rooster to guard the henhouse. He isn't even fully grown yet. Once he is, he'll be a fine protector for our hens."

"But, Daddy, he's mean to me! Please make him go away."

"You like having eggs for breakfast, right?"

"Yeah, but roosters don't lay eggs." I puffed out my chest and lifted my chin.

"True, but a good rooster can chase off a weasel or other animal that might try to eat our chickens. Without our chickens, we have no eggs. Do you understand?"

"Yes, Daddy. I understand, but can't we just get a nice rooster?" Tears spilled over my cheeks.

"No, Beth. The rooster stays. Just don't go near him, and you'll be fine." He sat back in his chair and opened his newspaper.

I didn't dare argue, but I knew my dad was wrong. I felt it in my bones. The next afternoon, my knowledge was confirmed.

I looked out the screen door to make sure the devil rooster was nowhere around. I opened the old door as quietly as I could manage and closed it behind me with barely a sound. I crept across the yard to my bicycle and pushed it to the end of our driveway at the top of the hill. I looked around once again before climbing onto my bike and pushing down on the pedal. The tires had rolled one rotation before I heard, "EER EER EER EER EER!"

That devil rooster had been lying in wait for me behind the barn. I pedaled as fast as I could, but he caught me. He slashed at my bare legs and pecked at my ankles. I screamed for all I was worth. My big brother, Toby, dashed out of the house letting the door bang shut behind him.

"What in the world is going on here?" he yelled.

"He's trying to eat me!" I cried as he pecked at my ankle again. The wounds were bleeding freely, but I didn't dare stop to look at them.

Toby grabbed a stick and swung it at the rooster. "Get outta here, you stupid bird! Get!"

The rooster took off toward the barn with his hackles still raised.

"Geez, Beth, he got you good. What'd you do to him?" He put the stick down and helped me off my bike.

I couldn't answer him because I was sobbing in great hiccupping breaths. All I could do was run to the house and find Mom.

"Good gracious, what happened to you, Beth?" Mom sat me down at the kitchen table and grabbed a cloth to clean my gashes and slashes.

"The rooster got her," Toby answered for me. He was a good brother sometimes.

Mom took my chin in her hand and made

me look her in the eyes. "What did you do to the rooster? Tell me the truth now."

"I didn't do anything. I pushed my bike to the end of the driveway and rode it back down. I didn't even see him until he started chasing me." My tears were slowing down and my breathing was getting easier.

"Are you telling me that chicken chased you without any reason?" Mom asked. She cocked her head in the way that told me she thought I was lying to her.

"Yes! He's mean! Make him go away!" I balled my hands into fists so tight my knuckles turned white.

"No more of this nonsense. You were told to leave the rooster alone. Now, don't go near him again, or you'll be grounded." She grunted and went back to doing the laundry.

Toby shrugged his shoulders and mumbled, "Sorry, Sis," before going to his room.

Left alone in the kitchen, all I could think about was how unfair this was. The mean bird attacked me, and I was going to get punished if it happened again? That just didn't make sense. I wondered what would happen if the rooster attacked one of them. I didn't wait long to find out.

That evening, Mom and Dad decided to go for a walk after dinner. They meandered up the hill toward the end of the driveway whispering to each other. Mom would occasionally giggle, so Dad must've been telling her all kinds of funny jokes.

They'd just reached the top of the hill when that devil rooster ran straight for them. He crowed, raised his hackles, flapped his wings, and extended his talons. He nearly got Mom, but Dad swung a leg out just in time to protect her. The rooster rounded on Dad and pecked at his ankles as my parents ran back to the house like the hounds of hell were on their tails. Mom was screaming, Dad was yelling, and the devil rooster was giving them both what for.

I had run into the house when I saw the rooster and watched the whole thing from the safety of a closed screen door. I moved out of the way so Mom and Dad could run in the house and slam the door.

"That stupid bird attacked us out of nowhere! We didn't do a thing to him. We didn't even look at him!" Mom paced the living room ringing her hands. "He's dangerous, George."

Dad nodded and turned to me. "Beth, we

owe you an apology. We didn't believe that you weren't teasing the rooster. We're sorry." He reached out for me and gathered me into his warm embrace.

Mom stood close and stroked my hair. "That mean old bird is never going to chase you again, Beth. We promise."

"What are you going to do with him?" I sniffled.

"Don't you worry about that," Dad said. "He's going away, just like you asked."

The next day, I pushed my bike to the top of the hill at the end of the driveway and rode all the way to the house without anything chasing me. Then I got brave and rode the bike back up the hill before speeding down again. My healing legs pumped easily and propelled me to speeds that must surely rival race cars.

That evening we all sat down to dinner, and I was so happy to see that Mom had made my favorite food −fried chicken.

ONE FOGGY NIGHT

Fog clung to the country road in thick clouds as Nikki drove home from her mother's house. Weariness weighed on her shoulders from spending the entire day scrapbooking. She contemplated the project she and her mother had embarked upon as she navigated the winding road. With hundreds of pictures that needed sorted and labeled, she wasn't sure how they were supposed to get everything ready for family viewing by Christmas.

Lost in her thoughts, she didn't see the large buck running across the road in front of her. She slammed on her brakes and turned the wheel sharply to the right. She missed the deer, but there was no shoulder on the steep hill.

The seatbelt tightened, snapping her into place as her airbag deployed. As it rolled down the hill like a child's toy to the valley below, she could see only dust from the airbag and hear the sickening creaking and crunching of her car's body being destroyed.

Silence filled the air when the car finally came to a stop, and for a moment Nikki thought she must have perished. After the dust settled a bit, she performed a mental survey of her body noting several cuts, scrapes, and some pain where the safety belt had tightened across her chest, but nothing life-threatening. Slowly disentangling herself from the safety equipment, she turned off the key and forced her car door open.

Perusing her surroundings, she could see only darkness. An attempt to use her cell phone to call for help proved there was no service in the valley. Taking a deep breath for courage, she got moving.

She realized the hill back up to the road was too steep to climb. Walking through the valley in search of a likely place for a phone or a location where she had service was the only option. Reasoning that she might be miles from the nearest house, and her car would be invisible in this thick fog, she hastened her steps. She was thankful her cell phone's flashlight app provided a little light.

She shivered from the cold as the drizzle soaked through her clothes. She didn't want her husband, Tom, to find her frozen dead body in the morning. She forced herself to keep going with a determination to survive.

Just as Nikki was about to give in to her overwhelming urge to cry, she spotted a faint light in the distance. Hurrying toward the source of light, she was overcome with relief when she saw a small cabin. A thin plume of smoke curled from the chimney as the flame from a hurricane lamp danced in the window. She said a quick prayer that the cabin was not inhabited by an ax murderer and knocked softly.

The door eased open to reveal a pleasant looking middle-aged woman dressed in a red vintage house dress and bright red lipstick. She looked like an older version of Nikki with her dark hair braided in one thick rope that reached her waist and dark brown eyes shining in her pleasant round face.

She looked like an angel as she asked,

"Are you lost, dear?"

"Actually," Nikki began in a wobbly voice, "I just had a car accident and was hoping to use your phone to call for help."

The lady opened the door wider and beckoned her inside. "It must be thirty degrees out there, and you are soaked to the skin! Come inside and warm yourself for a bit. We'll see if we can find a phone after you stop shivering. I'm afraid I don't have one, and the nearest neighbor is a good five miles away."

Hesitating for only a moment, she entered the cozy cabin. "Thank you very much." She pressed close to the antique pot belly stove in the living room, soaking up the blissful warmth. "My name's Nikki, and I sure do appreciate your kindness."

"Not at all, dear!" the woman cried. "You can call me Lizzie. My goodness, you look like you got a little banged up. Have a seat by the fire, and I'll fetch some iodine."

Too exhausted to argue, she sank down into an antique rocking chair near the stove. She sighed as the wood heat seeped into her body, easing the ache from her limbs.

Lizzie soon returned with iodine, a wash cloth, a small kettle of water, and a cup holding tea bag. They chatted as Lizzie cleaned the worst of Nikki's cuts and scratches while the tea steeped on the stove until Lizzie deemed it ready.

"No home remedy is complete without a cup of hot tea," Lizzie insisted. "It will warm your bones and calm your spirit."

Sipping the hot tea, she listened to Lizzie's stories about how her children were always suffering from some injury or another when they were small, and how much she missed them since they grew up and moved away.

Succumbing to exhaustion, she fell asleep in the rocking chair with the empty tea cup still in her hand. She thought she felt someone remove the cup, cover her with a blanket, and kiss her on the forehead just before she drifted off completely, but she wasn't certain.

The next morning, Nikki awoke in her car where it had come to rest in the valley. She looked around in confusion, wondering if she had dreamed everything about Lizzie and the little cabin. Adding to her confusion, she felt inexplicably warm, considering the car was covered in a thin layer of ice.

She sat stunned for a moment when she

realized that she was snuggled under a red and white hand-made quilt that she had never seen before. The airbag was deflated enough to allow for easy movement. A glance in the rear-view mirror revealed lip prints on her forehead where someone wearing bright red lipstick had kissed her.

She looked all around but could find no logical explanation for the quilt or the lipstick. Trying to make sense of the night before, Nikki was startled by someone knocking on her car window. She turned toward the sound to find her worried husband attempting to open the car door. She practically ripped the door off its hinges getting out and jumping into his arms.

"I was so worried about you!" Tom whispered, holding her tightly.

"How in the world did you find me?" Nikki asked, taking in his pale face, lined with worry and dark half-moon circles beneath his blue eyes.

"I drove up and down all of the roads between our house and your mom's for most of the night. I was just about to call all of our family and friends when I saw that I'd missed a call. A woman left a voicemail telling me exactly where to find you. She didn't leave a name, and I didn't recognize her voice. I'm just happy she called."

After being rescued, she caught a few hours of sleep and a hot shower. Waking up feeling good enough to help her mother scrapbook some more, they moved the project to Nikki's house. She caught her breath as she lifted one particular photo.

"Mom, who is this person? Where is that cabin?" The thundering of her heart made it difficult to breathe.

Nikki's mom looked at the photo. "That's my grandma. Her name was Elizabeth, but everyone called her Lizzie. That's the cabin where she lived most of her life. She died when I was a baby, so I don't remember her. I do know that her favorite color was red." A small smile brightened her face. "She loved her red lipstick."

"My mother always said Grandma felt like a movie star in her red lipstick. The older folks still talked about it when I was a little girl because they thought such a color was scandalous. I bet she's even wearing it in that picture, but you can't tell because it's in black and white. You look quite a bit like her."

Nikki felt faint as she whispered, "That's

the woman who saved me, and she's standing in front of the cabin where I spent the night."

Her mom patted her hand. "No one has lived in that cabin in many years, and you spent the night in your car, honey. Maybe you aren't up for this project today, after all. I'll just get out of here, so you can get some rest."

Later that afternoon, Nikki drove Tom's truck to the crash site and searched the area. She was sore from her accident, but she was determined to find proof of her sanity.

After searching for about an hour, she located the remains of a cabin. A small piece of one wall was still standing, but the rest had been reduced to a pile of rubble. She dug through the debris, searching for something – what, she didn't know. She moved some boards and beneath them found the old pot belly stove lying on its side, partially sunken into the earth. It was covered in the dirt and debris of many years, but she was absolutely certain she had found the right place.

Nikki stood looking at the stove and the remains of the cabin for a long time before she whispered, "Thank you, Grandma

Lizzie."

The wind suddenly picked up, and Nikki swore she heard the whispered reply, "You are welcome, Baby Girl."

Grandma Dottie's
Secret Recipes

Climbing the front porch steps to her cousin's house, Zoe let out a breath. While Alyssa was her closest living relative, she didn't have much in common with the young woman. She couldn't imagine what had possessed her cousin to invite her over.

Alyssa swung the door wide at her knock, cell phone in hand.

"Oh, hey. Come on in. I've been cleaning Mom's house out so I can sell it. I found some stuff for you. I know you like musty old books, so here you go. I think those are journals or something. They're written in cursive, so I can't be sure." She sneered at the large dusty box on the floor. "I don't know why anyone ever thought that was a good way to write stuff down."

She regarded her young cousin in surprise. "Can't you read cursive? I learned it in third grade."

Alyssa shook her head. "Nope. Everything is on computer now. The school didn't teach us because we don't need it like you did in the olden days." She held up a hand to stop Zoe from responding. "Before you say anything about history, everything worth knowing is online."

Zoe was overwhelmed by a wave of sadness at the cavalier statement. She and her cousin were from different generations, and it was obvious in every aspect of their lives.

"I'm only forty, you know. It's not like the dinosaurs were still around when I was in school. It wasn't that long ago." She opened one of the top flaps of the box to reveal several beautiful old leather notebooks in various colors. "Where did you get these?"

"I found them in Mom's attic when I was digging through the house. Damien wanted to throw them away, but I know how much you love old things nobody else wants, especially if they're books. I called you instead."

She tamped down her instinct to be snarky and smiled. "Thank you for thinking of me and not letting your boyfriend throw away family heirlooms. I do love dusty old things."

Alyssa was already on her phone checking social media, probably posting about how she recycled old junk by giving it to the needy. It was one of her favorite white lies.

Gritting her teeth, Zoe forced herself to be polite. "Thanks again. I'll see you later."

She didn't know if her cousin heard her or not, but she hefted the large, dusty box of books and saw herself out. Placing the box in the backseat of her car, she started to get excited.

Curiosity mingled with delight inside her during her drive home. She couldn't wait to see what was written in those books. She'd once seen some old farm ledgers that one of her ancestors had kept. She'd loved reading about the fluctuation of corn prices in the 1940s. It was a window into her forefather's life.

Lugging her burden into her house, she placed it on the kitchen table with great reverence. She poured herself a tall glass of iced tea and wiped off the box with a clean cloth. Then she removed each book inside with the greatest of care, cleaning each one in turn. When everything was free of loose particles, she washed her hands and picked up the first book.

The small, black leather book did look like a journal at first glance. Opening it to the first page, she gasped at what she read. This book was a treasure beyond measure. The first page bore the name, Dottie Ellison. Beneath her name was written, "Top Secret Recipes." She'd just discovered her great-grandmother's secret recipe book. As she looked through the rest of the journals, she discovered they were all filled with recipes and stories from her great-grandma's life.

Turning each page with the utmost care, Zoe read all about Grandma Dottie's culinary adventures. She had loved entering the county fair and church cooking competitions every year. She'd made notes on what the judges had said, what her competition had presented, and how she could improve the recipe. Thumbing through the pages, she felt herself smiling.

She caught her breath as she settled on one page. Grandma Dottie's Coconut Meringue Pie. She hadn't seen this recipe since Christmas dinner when she was a kid. As she read the notes, she saw that her grandma used an unusual ingredient in that recipe.

The Best Ever Flour Company Bake Off deadline was coming up soon, but she had time to test the recipe. The pie turned out better than she'd ever dreamed. Flaky crust, creamy filling bursting with flavor, and meringue so perky it could only be called perfect.

She entered the contest mere minutes before the deadline. Feeling good about her entry, she went about her daily tasks anxious to hear something. Joy zinged through her when she received the call that she was a top-ten finalist and would bake her pie for the championship on live TV.

The venue in Charlotte, North Carolina, home of Best Ever Flour Company was all decked out with fun decorations, but the other contestants looked fierce. Celebrity TV Chef, Ruby Sterling was one of the judges, and the atmosphere reminded her of a circus. People were fawning all over the cooking star and running around in every direction.

Zoe stepped into her kitchen area with nerves so frazzled they were making her head buzz. Pushing through it, she concentrated on what she was doing. As she beat the egg whites for the meringue, cream of tartar, sugar, and vanilla, her thoughts lingered on Grandma Dottie.

She remembered her with great love, but the memories were like objects hidden in mist. Sometimes she could make one out and sometimes she only got an outline and a vague impression. The one thing she remembered clear as water was her great-grandmother's prowess in the kitchen. No one could touch the quality of her food. No one could bake a pie nearly as delicious. She let her memories take her mind from the pressure of competition and became attuned to her creation.

Her pie was the loveliest she'd ever baked. She presented it to the judges with the pride of a schoolgirl who'd just mastered something new. Ruby zoned in on it immediately. She approached with a friendly smile.

"Tell me, how do you think you did?" she asked.

Swallowing the lump in her throat, Zoe found her voice. "I believe I did well. I did my best, so it has to be good enough."

Ruby laughed; the sound soft like the purr of a contented kitten. "Well, you can't do any better than that. I look forward to trying your pie."

TV cameras zoomed in and out as the judges tasted everything and conferred with each other. After what felt like days of deliberation, the host announced they had a winner.

The celebrity judge walked to the center of the stage and gazed at all of the contestants. She said something nice about everyone's entry. When it was Zoe's turn, she complimented the perfect coconut flavor and outstanding meringue.

"And the winner of the $20,000 grand prize is Zoe Ellison for Grandma Dottie's Coconut Meringue Pie!"

The crowd erupted in applause, and the other contestants pretended to be happy for her. The rest of the afternoon was a blur.

After the crowd dispersed and everyone

went home, Zoe sat in her hotel room mesmerized by her check. The large one for her wall was nice, but the small slip of paper in her hand meant the end of her financial woes. She finally had enough money to pay off her debt and buy herself a new bookshelf. The one she'd duct taped together so many times could finally rest in pieces. She owed it all to her long-deceased great-grandmother and a self-absorbed cousin who couldn't read cursive.

Should she share some of the prize money with Alyssa since she was the one who gave her Grandma Dottie's book? It would be a kind gesture, but she nearly threw the books away without caring what was in them. She hadn't so much as texted to see what the journals said.

Contemplating the right thing to do, Zoe realized that if Alyssa had kept the books, she could never have enjoyed them. Worse, all of the recipes would have been lost. Her idea struck her with such force that she had to sit down. She could do something for her cousin and home bakers everywhere. She had eight months to make it happen. Delighted with her decision, she opened her laptop and began researching.

That Christmas, she presented a box wrapped in gold paper to her cousin. Alyssa ripped it open without much enthusiasm, her phone dangling from her finger by its ring holder. That changed when she turned the gift over and peered at the front.

Alyssa put her phone down on the table beside her and studied Zoe as though seeing her for the first time. "What is this? *Grandma Dottie's Secret Recipes, Compiled by Zoe Ellison*. Dottie was our great-grandmother. How did you get her recipes?"

Wiping a tear from her cheek, Zoe cleared her throat. "You gave them to me. Those leather journals you gave me were filled with her recipes. I put them together in a cookbook so you can enjoy them, too."

She laughed, wiping a few of her own tears. "I had no idea those books were so precious. I almost let Damien trash them." She took Zoe's hand. "Thank you. You have no idea how much this means to me."

"There's actually a little more to it. I published the book worldwide, and I'm splitting the royalties with you. The treasures hidden in those books belong to both of us."

Alyssa grinned. "Thanks, Zoe. I know

you and I are really different people, but deep down where it counts, we're the same because we're family."

A Terrible Neighbor

I pressed the doorbell and studied the yellow Victorian home. Thankful the covered porch protected me from the rain, I watched a slight figure lumber forward through the heavy mahogany door's leaded glass window.

"Yes?" Her short silver hair reflected the light behind her, giving her the illusion of a halo.

"I'm Detective Darlene Anderson with Springfield Police Department. I'm here to ask a few questions about your neighbor." I studied her reactions as I spoke. Her eyes had widened a fraction before she schooled her features.

"I'm Grace Mills." She extended her hand. "Please come inside."

I followed her into an old-fashioned parlor with rose-colored wall paper. "This is a lovely home," I said and eased into a gold wingback chair.

"Thank you, dear. I was born and raised here. Moved back after my parents passed." She settled into my chair's mate, facing me. "Which neighbor would you like to discuss?"

"Marla Wilson, your next-door neighbor to the east." I took out my notepad and a pen. "Have you noticed anything unusual at her place lately?"

She stiffened. "Why do you ask? I hope she's not in any trouble."

"We're trying to locate her. She missed a lunch date with her daughter, Stacy, who hasn't been able to reach her for a couple of days. Can you tell me when you saw her last?" I poised my pen above my paper, keeping a close eye on her.

She sniffed. "If you've spoken with Stacy, then you know Marla and I aren't friendly."

I made a note. "Why is that?"

"We have a disagreement over her

driveway. She had it poured on my property, but she insists it's on hers." The old woman's spine couldn't have been more rigid if it was made of rebar. "I haven't seen her lately. She keeps company with several men. Perhaps you should ask one of them."

I jotted a note to look into the feud and multiple partners. "How many?"

She fisted her hands. "At least three."

"Can you tell me anything about these men? Names? Descriptions? What they drive?"

She huffed. "I don't watch. I just see them coming and going at different times. It's disgraceful. That sort of trash lowers property values and sullies the reputation of the good people of this neighborhood."

"Has she been keeping company like this for long?"

"Off and on for years. Poor Stacy probably doesn't even know who her father is."

Wind and rain pounded the window panes as the storm picked up strength. Thunderclaps rattled the glass in their wooden frames. "Looks like this storm is getting worse. Do you have someplace safe?" I asked.

She stood. "Yes, I have shelter. You probably need to get back to your station. I'm sure you have work there."

"Just a couple more questions. When did you last see anyone at Marla's?"

She hissed out a breath. "Saturday. She was watering her plants in a pair of skimpy shorts."

"How long have you been neighbors?"

"Since I moved back ten years ago. She bought her house when Mother was still here."

"Did your mother get along with her?"

"Yes, she even had her over for tea upon occasion. Mother had such a friendly nature." She patted her silver curls and swung the door open. "Drive safely, Detective."

I stepped out into the storm. Trees bowed under the wind's ferocity. Raindrops pelted my skin like the sting of angry insects.

Running to the car, I slid in the mud, spinning toward the house with my momentum. A fork of lightning flashed across the sky, lighting the world, and giving me a view of a silhouette through the basement window.

I crept closer, about to peek inside for a

better look when the lights came on, and I heard a loud WHACK.

"You've caused me a lot of trouble. A policewoman was here nosing around. It's all your fault, harlot!"

I peered through the window and saw Grace holding a thick leather belt in front of a woman tied to a chair. Wearing pink shorts and a blood-smeared white tank top, every inch of her bare skin was covered in bloody welts and bruises. Stringy blond hair covered most of her face and a dirty gag kept her from calling out. No doubt about it, I'd found Marla.

I radioed for backup and raced to the door where I pounded. "Police! Open Up!"

When nobody answered, I tried the knob, which was unlocked. As the storm raged, I opened doors until I found the basement. I took the steps two at a time, my taser drawn. When I reached the bottom, Grace spun toward me, belt held high.

"You should've gone back to your station. Now you've rudely interrupted me, and you're dripping water on my floor. Disgraceful!" Her bulging eyes sparkled with insanity. She motioned to a bench along a wall. "Sit down over there. Handcuff yourself to the bench. I'll deal with you later."

"You don't understand the situation," I said. "I have a taser and won't hesitate to use it. Put the belt down and your hands behind your head."

"No. I'm tired of trashy harlots running amok. It isn't proper!"

We circled each other like boxers, each waiting to see what the other would do. Once I was close enough to the bound woman, I glanced at her. I was shocked to see the gag's knot, stuffed into her mouth, was the size of a tennis ball. Keeping my attention on Grace, I reached over with my free hand and worked the rag out of her mouth.

Marla, rasped, "Crazy old bat!"

Grace swung the belt at her victim, and I deployed my taser. She dropped to the ground shaking and screeching. My backup arrived in time to tend to her while I untied Marla.

"I'm Detective Darlene Anderson. Are you okay? Can you tell me what happened?"

Her voice was rough as jagged rocks by the sea. "She tricked me."

"Paramedics are coming," said an officer

behind me.

"Thanks." I glanced up and saw him dragging a handcuffed Grace toward the stairs.

Someone gave me a bottle of water, which I tried to give to Marla. When she showed me her bloody hands, I lifted the bottle to her lips. "How did she trick you?"

"I was outside watering my plants. She came over and apologized for the trouble. Invited me over for tea. I thought it was a peace offering"

I gave her another sip. "And then?"

"When I got here, she asked me to get a jar of honey from the basement. Lots of people store food in the basement, so I thought nothing of it."

"What happened when you got down here?"

"She whacked me on the head, knocking me out. I woke up to her hitting me with a belt and calling me a harlot."

I heard paramedics thundering down the stairs and told Marla, "Medical help is here. Besides Stacy, is there anyone you'd like contacted?"

"My three brothers. They've been helping me fix up my house to sell. They're probably worried."

I hadn't seen that coming. "You're selling your house?"

"Yeah. The neighborhood went downhill when Grace moved in. She's a terrible neighbor."

GWEN'S USED BOOKS

———— ❧ ————

Lightning forked across the sky as Gwen wiped sweat from her forehead. The hair on her arms stood up with the storm's electricity. Hefting the last box from her car, she struggled to balance her heavy burden. She hauled her latest acquisition inside and set it on the counter, locking the door behind her.

"Well, that's the last one, Athena. None too soon, either." She smiled at her best friend and store mascot, her beloved white Chihuahua.

Athena lifted her head from her yellow beanbag behind the counter. Cocking her ears forward, she let out a huff of air and rested her chin on her paws.

Gwen shook her head. "Good talk, Athena. Now let's get down to business. What treasures did the late Harold Rumbottom have tucked away in these dusty old boxes?"

Extending the blade of her retractable utility knife, she ran the tip across the ancient brown tape sealing the first box. The scent of musty books filled her lungs before she opened the flap. Her hands shook at the sight of the old tomes cocooned within the battered cardboard.

The box was filled with all sorts of books. She'd anticipated finding some Shakespeare, but she hadn't expected all of the wonderful fairy tales. She dusted a volume of Hans Christian Andersen's *Complete Fairy Tales and Short Stories* with her lint-free cloth. She placed it on the counter beside Shakespeare's *A Midsummer Night's Dream* and reached into the box for another book.

Rain pelted the windows like angry wasps demanding entry by the time she reached for the last book. Using both hands, she lifted a thick brown leather-bound tome bearing no discernable title. After running her cloth over the cover, Gwen eased the book open.

A puff of green smoke gushed into her face, stinging her eyes and throat. Struggling to breathe, she wasn't prepared when Athena leapt up and knocked the book from her hands. The dog's fierce snarls vibrated her entire body.

Gwen tried to retrieve the book from the floor, but Athena batted her hand away. "What's wrong with you?"

Her fierce protector yipped in response. She lowered her head and growled at the book, her hackles standing straight up.

"Athena!" Gwen picked her up and held her like a football beneath one arm while she reached for the book with her other hand. "What's gotten in to you?"

"I'm afraid it's me," said a voice from behind her.

She squealed and spun around, losing her grip on Athena and abandoning the book. The dog landed in a run, rushing over to the tall well-dressed stranger with salt and pepper hair, trying to attack his ankles. Her head passed right through him.

"Who are you? How did you get in here? What do you want?"

"Elizabeth? Is that you?" He glided

toward her.

She took a step back and held her hands up in front of her as she'd been taught in self-defense class. "No. I'm Gwen. Now tell me who you are and how you got into my store."

"Please excuse the intrusion. The resemblance between you and my Elizabeth is striking. You've the same fair skin. The same wild dark hair. You even have the same boldness in your brown eyes." He shook his head.

"I'm sorry, but I don't know your Elizabeth."

"My apologies. She was my daughter. You are her mirror image. Perhaps you're one of her descendants." He extended his hand as if for a handshake. "My name is Peter, and I've been imprisoned in yonder book for quite some time. I owe you a debt of gratitude for releasing me."

She scooped up Athena and backed further away from the stranger. "What are you? You aren't solid."

"Sadly, I am no longer flesh and blood. I've been a spirit for a long time."

"You said you were imprisoned inside

that book." She pointed to the tome on the floor. "How did that happen?"

"It's a long story, but if you've the time, I'll share it with you."

Gwen glanced at the dog in her arms who was keeping a suspicious eye on the phantom. "I have some time." She settled on a stool and held her best friend to her chest.

"Well, where to begin?" A beautiful clay pipe appeared in his hand, and he took a long puff. "Ah yes. You see, I always loved books. In my time, bookstores were great meeting places."

"When was your time?"

"I was born in 1838. I met my demise in 1888." He chuckled. "I'd lost the energy of youth but not the curiosity."

"What happened?"

"One thing at a time, my dear. Now, where was I? Oh, yes. I died on the sideway in front of my favorite bookstore. I couldn't seem to move on, so I haunted the store. It was nice at first. I had all the time in the world to wander around the store with the customers. I listened to their conversations and felt content. I loved spending my days close to all those beautiful books. The trouble was I couldn't pick them up and read them. Every time I tried to grasp a book, it slipped through my fingers to the floor."

"How did you die?" she asked.

He took a long puff from his pipe. Purple smoke wafted through the air followed by the sweet scent of pipe tobacco. "I felt a horrible pressure in my chest and couldn't breathe. I fell to the ground and awoke as a ghost. Now, please stop interrupting me."

"I'm sorry." She rose and put Athena, who'd nearly been lulled to sleep by Peter's voice, on her beanbag before retaking her seat.

"The shopkeeper wasn't pleased with my continued mess. I must admit, I left several books strewn around the space every night. It took him a while to clean up of a morning so he could open. Before I truly understood how annoyed he was, he brought in a shaman. I wasn't worried at first, but this fellow was quite powerful. He set a diabolical trap for me."

"The book." Color drained from Gwen's face with the realization.

"Yes. He left that beautiful volume on the counter. I couldn't see a title and was ever so curious. I tried to grasp the book, which fell to the floor. This one was different, though. It landed open. When I leaned over to examine it, I was sucked inside. The shaman returned the next day, closed the book, and whispered an incantation over it. I couldn't understand what he said."

Taking a hanky from his pocket, the ghost wiped his brow. "That shopkeeper was Sebastian Rumbottom. He locked me away in a wooden box. He passed it to his son, and his son after him, and so on. Each generation was warned to keep the book locked up and never open it. I heard the warning with each and every passing of my book."

"So, you were aware of your surroundings?"

"That was the worst part. I could hear everything, but it was so dark and cold. I heard bits and pieces from so many lives, but no one ever talked to me. I was so very lonely."

Someone pounded on the door hard enough the art on the walls shook. Gwen turned to see the oldest of the Rumbottom descendants, her high school sweetheart, through the glass.

"You'd better hide. I have a feeling he's come for you."

"I won't go back in that book!" He fled to the Reference Section in the back of the store.

Forcing out a nervous breath, Gwen unlocked the glass door. "Sam, come in. What brings you out on such a stormy night?"

He shook some of the water from his jacket and wiped the rain from his eyes. "I think we sold you an heirloom by mistake. I'm here to buy it back from you."

"Oh, of course. What's this heirloom you're looking for? I've only unpacked one box, so I probably haven't found it yet."

"It's a thick brown leather book. It wasn't supposed to be packed away in some flimsy cardboard. I don't know what my dad was thinking." He glanced around the shop.

"I've seen several brown leather books. What's the title?"

"There isn't one. It's a special book to the family, but it wouldn't be of interest to anyone else." He sidled up to the counter and examined each of the books.

"Are there any distinguishing marks that would help me identify it?" She moved to block the tome from view with her body.

Sam shook his head. "No. It's extremely

important that I find it." He held her gaze. "I don't want to alarm you, but the book is dangerous. I need to take it back home where I can keep an eye on it."

An agonized screech rent the air. Gwen looked up to see Peter flying straight for Sam. "Peter, no! What are you doing?"

"I won't go back in that prison! I never did anything to your family. I don't deserve to be locked away."

Sam glared at her. "I see you've already found it. Is he the only one you let out?"

She rose to her full height, propping her hands on her hips. "You mean there are more spirits locked inside that book? Why would anyone do that?"

"Not necessarily spirits, but there are many things locked inside that volume. Now, I need to know how many you set free."

"I've only seen Peter. I opened the cover to try to find the title, and green smoke rushed out at me. Then he appeared."

He regarded the ghost. "You must be the bookstore phantom. Do you know if any of the others escaped?"

"I was utterly alone in that book. If there were others, they never said a word to me."

"Sam, please explain this to me. How is this even possible?"

He sighed. "Gwen, I need to get the book closed. Peter was trapped in there by accident. My ancestor was trying to catch a demon that had been sniffing around. The shaman assured him they'd caught the right creature, but apparently not."

He turned to Peter. "My great, great-grandfather didn't mind you wandering around his store. He actually missed you once you were gone."

"Then why did he leave me in there all these years? Why did you?"

"Try to understand. There are twelve demons and evil creatures trapped within the pages of that magic book. You were Number Thirteen. Such books can only hold thirteen entities, so it was locked away to protect the world until a way could be found to safely return them to their realm."

"Have you found a way yet?" Gwen crossed her arms over her chest with a frown.

"I think so, but I haven't tested my theory yet. It's urgent I get the book out of here now." His eyes blazed and sweat beaded on his forehead.

"Okay, you can take the book, but leave Peter here. He can haunt my store until he's ready to move on. He deserves that much."

Sam smiled. "You're right. You always did have a big loving heart. It's one of the things I loved about you."

Old tender feelings threatened to resurface at that small admission, but Gwen tamped them down. Sam was far too pushy for her and had knowingly left poor Peter trapped.

He turned to the ghost. "Peter, I'm sorry for what happened to you. I'd like to come back and visit you later if that's okay. I'd love to talk to you about your life and the people you knew."

The dapper ghost straightened his suit jacket. "That should be fine, my boy."

Sam nodded, scooped the book off the floor, and headed out into the storm.

"Do you believe him?" Gwen asked.

"I believe that's what the young man was told, but there are no demons or anything else in that book. I spent over a hundred and thirty years in there by myself. I think Sebastian's shaman may have exaggerated his skills."

"I'm glad you're finally free. Sam will

figure things out sooner or later. He's a smart guy. You're welcome to stay here for as long as you like."

Her unexpected guest bowed at the waist. "Thank you, Gwen. It's good to finally be home. I shall endeavor to keep the mess to a minimum."

Gwen smiled. "I'll start coming in a little early. We'll see what we can do about making it a little easier for you to read. We can experiment with an e-reader. I've heard spirits can manipulate electronics."

The ghost's brows puckered in confusion. "What the devil is an e-reader?"

"One of many things you'll learn about. Welcome to the twenty-first century, Peter. I think you'll like it here."

YELLOW BICYCLE

"I don't need a bicycle, Mrs. Wentworth," Jade told the woman trying to push the bike through her front door.

"I'm moving into a senior apartment, and I can't take it with me. Please, you must keep it for me. You're the only one who'll care for it properly." She leaned on the faded yellow Schwinn.

"This is a kid's bike. I don't have kids. What would I do with it?" Jade shook her head.

"My son will throw it away. He doesn't understand it's important." Tears streamed down the old woman's face while her eyes pleaded.

Jade's heart twisted. "Come inside, and we'll talk about it." She opened the door wide and stepped aside. "Would you like a cup of coffee?"

"Yes, please." Propping the bike against the wall, she settled herself at the kitchen table.

"So, what's so special about this bicycle?" She handed Mrs. Wentworth a cup of coffee and sat down across from her.

The old woman sighed and wiped the tears from her weathered cheeks. "It was Lizzie's."

"Oh," Jade said softly. "I'm so sorry. I had no idea it was your daughter's bike. I've never seen it before. Are you sure Tom doesn't want it? It was his sister's, after all."

She shook her head. "No. Tom refuses to talk about her after what happened. He won't even speak her name. He wants to forget he ever had a sister. He sure doesn't want anything that belonged to her." The old mother sobbed.

Jade patted her hand. "I'll keep the bike. It's no problem. Maybe I'll hang it on the wall."

"She would like that. Thank you," Mrs.

Wentworth whispered.

"She?" Jade asked with a frown.

"Lizzie. She would like the bike hung on your wall."

She paused at the lady's odd words. "How old was your daughter when she had her accident?"

"It was no accident!" Mrs. Wentworth shouted. She took a deep breath and continued. "I'm sorry. I didn't mean to yell at you. Someone pushed her off that bridge. She was nine years old. They didn't even look for who did it." She hid her face in her hands, sobs wracking her body.

Jade stood and wrapped the old woman in a warm embrace until she calmed.

"She's been gone thirty years. I've kept the bike in her bedroom, but I can't care for her anymore."

"It's okay. I'll take good care of it for you. There's no need to worry," Jade whispered.

"Thank you, dear. Don't let Tom have it if he asks. Promise me you'll keep Lizzie's bike."

Jade nodded. "I promise. I'll leave it right here in the kitchen until I find a proper place for it."

"That's good. Thank you. You've always been a sweet girl. My Lizzie would have been your best friend if she'd lived." She sighed and stood. "I should get back home. Will you visit me in my new apartment? I'll be at Golden Towers in 13D."

"Of course, I'll visit. We've been neighbors for so long that we're almost family." She smiled and continued. "Who else will help me eat the chocolate chip cookies I like to bake?"

Mrs. Wentworth ambled to the door, then turned and hugged Jade. "You're a good person. I turn over guardianship to you with confidence."

She tilted her head in confusion. "Guardianship?"

The old woman patted her shoulder. "I'll be seeing you, Jade. Tom's moving me to the old folks' home in the morning. I'll miss you."

"I'll miss you, too. Are you sure you really want to move?"

"Tom doesn't have time to keep up my yard and deal with things that need tending around the house. I'm afraid I'm not able to do much of my own home upkeep anymore." Mrs. Wentworth sighed. "Tom's probably right. It's for the best."

"I'll come visit soon, and you can give me the grand tour."

She smiled and patted Jade's cheek. "You're a good girl. I look forward to your visit."

Jade closed the door with a soft click and leaned against it. Lizzie's death had been a tragedy. The little girl was riding her bike home from a friend's house, but never arrived. The bike had been discovered on a bridge, and her body was found a mile downriver.

"Why are you crying?"

Jade jumped and screeched at the girl's voice. "Who's there?"

"Mommy said you're going to take care of me now because she has to move."

She looked toward the bicycle and saw the apparition of a little girl with blond pigtails. She was dressed in baby blue overalls adorned with pink hearts and a pink T-shirt.

Jade sank into a kitchen chair and dropped her head between her knees for a few heartbeats before looking at the ghost again. "Okay, you're still here. I'm not dreaming."

"You can't be dreaming. You're awake, silly."

She closed her eyes and opened them to see the little girl staring at her. "Hello. I'm Jade. And you are?"

The small ghost propped her fists on her hips and stuck out her lower lip. "I'm Lizzie. Duh. Who else would I be? My mom just brought me over to stay with you."

"I see. So, you came with the bicycle. That's what she meant about guardianship. She was talking about you. Please forgive me. I think I'm in shock."

Lizzie floated up to sit on the bike. "I guess I can see that. Mom was pretty shocked when I first talked to her, too. It really stinks that she can't keep me. She said you'd take good care of me."

"Um, sure I will. I wonder about something, though. Why are you here? It's been a long time since your accident. Why haven't you crossed over?"

"I dunno." She twirled a finger around one of her pigtails.

"Do you remember anything about what happened to you?"

She floated off the bike and over to the chair that Mrs. Wentworth had occupied just a few minutes before. "I was riding home from Becky's house. My bike chain slipped off the round thing with the teeth. I stopped and put it back on. I was about to get back on my bike when I felt someone push me from behind. I never saw who it was." She shrugged her translucent shoulders.

Jade scratched her head. "That must have been heart-breaking for your family. That's why your brother's behavior confuses me. Do you know why he wants to forget you? That seems a little odd."

"We had a big fight before I went to Becky's that day. He was mad because I ate his Fun Dip, and Mom let me go play anyway."

They were interrupted by a loud knock. Lizzie faded as Jade opened the door to reveal a scowling middle-aged man with thinning hair standing on her porch.

"Tom, what brings you here?" Jade blocked the entrance with her body.

"I understand Mom pushed that dumb old bike off on you. I've come to take it off your hands. There's no reason for you to deal with Mom's junk." He placed a foot on the threshold.

"I like the bike. I've decided to hang it on

my living room wall. Thanks for coming, though. Have a good night." She tried to close the door, but Tom grabbed it.

"I insist. That old relic needs to be recycled. It probably has lead paint on it. I wouldn't want you getting sick from lead exposure." He again tried to push his way inside.

"Why do you really want that bike? Is it because it was your sister's?"

His face paled and his lips flattened into a straight line. "That's none of your business. Technically, as the only heir to my mom's estate, that bike is mine."

Jade crossed her arms over her chest and set her feet. "Your mom is still alive. The heir doesn't receive property until after death. She asked me to take care of the bicycle. You can't have it."

"Jade, that bike must be destroyed!" He ran his fingers through his short brown hair.

Lizzie floated up beside Jade. "Why do you want to destroy my bike, Tommy?"

He stumbled off the porch and fell on his rear. "It can't be! Why are you here?"

"Something's keeping her here. She says she was pushed into the river. Do you know anything about that?"

Tom's face went from pale to red and sweat popped out of his forehead. "No. She fell off a bridge. It was just a stupid accident." His hands shook as he climbed to his feet.

"Are you sure? Why is it that you refuse to acknowledge you ever had a sister?"

His eyes bulged like a cornered animal. He leapt up the steps, pushing past Jade and the ghost. Grabbing the bike, he tried to yank the handle bars off.

"This must be destroyed! It must all be destroyed!"

Mrs. Wentworth appeared in the open doorway with a police officer. "I heard yelling and called the police. Tom, what are you doing? Put that down. It doesn't belong to you. I gave it to Jade."

"It's Lizzie's and must be destroyed!"

Jade's heart sank as she realized the truth. "Did you push Lizzie into the water that day?"

Tom sank down to the kitchen floor and dropped his head into his hands. He rocked back and forth. "No, no, no. It wasn't supposed to happen. She was just supposed to get all wet. She wasn't supposed to die."

Mrs. Wentworth fell to her knees. "You

pushed your sister?" she whispered.

"Mom, it was an accident. I was just getting her back for eating my candy. That's all."

The officer stepped forward. "Tom, I need you to come with me to the station. I'm placing you under arrest for the death of Elizabeth Wentworth."

He stood, straightened his shirt, and glared at Jade. "This is your fault. If you'd minded your own business, I could've destroyed that bike. Now I'll never be able to forget. I hate you for that."

The officer read Tom his rights and led him away, and Mrs. Wentworth turned to Jade with tears streaming down her cheeks. "My son killed my daughter. I don't know how to process something like this."

Jade wrapped her in a warm hug. "I don't know what to say."

Lizzie appeared at the old woman's side. "Mommy, it's okay. It wasn't your fault."

"My sweet Lizzie, I'm so sorry . . ." Mrs. Wentworth's frame shook with her sobs.

"Mommy, I hear Daddy calling me. It's time for me to go. He says we'll see you again. I love you." Lizzie vanished with those words.

"She's moved on to her reward." Jade handed her friend a tissue.

The old mother nodded and struggled to her feet. "Yes, and she says I'll see her and Marvin again. That makes me feel better."

Tears rolled down Jade's cheeks. "If you need anything at all, you just let me know."

"Thank you, dear. I suppose I'll need someone to help me move tomorrow since Tom's going to jail. I can't lift those heavy boxes I packed."

Jade shook her head. "Are you sure you want to move to that senior apartment? If it's just a matter of home maintenance, I can help you. I don't mind mowing your yard and helping you take care of your house. If you want to stay in your home, I'll do what I can to make that possible."

Mrs. Wentworth's eyes widened and a small smile formed on her lips. "You'd really do that for me?" Her shoulders slumped. "I can't ask you to do such a thing. I don't want to impose on you."

She held the lady's gaze. "I wouldn't have offered if I wasn't sincere. So, the question is simple. Where do you want to live?"

"I want to stay in my home. Marvin and I

bought that house fifty years ago. No apartment could ever be home in the same way."

Jade smiled. "Then it's settled. Call Golden Towers tomorrow and tell them you won't be moving in. I'll be over to help you unpack in the morning."

"Thank you, sweet child. You are a kind soul. I'll talk to you soon." Patting Jade's hand, she shuffled to the door. Without turning, she said, "I'd like for you to keep Lizzie's bike. Is that okay?"

"Of course. I'll hang it in the kitchen."

Over the next few years, Jade visited Mrs. Wentworth every day. She took care of the yard, the painting, and all of the holiday decorating. She made chocolate chip cookies while the grieving mother told stories about Lizzie's brief but beautiful childhood. The two became as close as any mother and daughter.

After Mrs. Wentworth joined Lizzie in the hereafter at the age of eighty, Jade received a certified letter from her lawyer. It stated that Mrs. Dorothy Wentworth had left her entire estate to one Jade McIntire. Among the holdings such as a house and car were several shares of stock in Dorel Industries, which owns Schwinn Bicycle Company.

LOST SHEEP

"**W**here are they? Where could they be?" Little Bo Peep wailed.

"When did you last see your sheep, Miss Peep?" Officer Wolfe asked.

"They were here in the meadow this morning. I left them alone for an hour while I had lunch with Little Red Riding Hood at Muffin Man's Café. Honestly, it was only an hour."

"Ah. I know the Muffin Man. He only serves the best food over on Drury Lane." Officer Wolfe adjusted his hat to shade more of his face. "Do your sheep have any distinguishing marks?"

"Yes, they all have pink ear tags."

He nodded and made some notes. "They most likely just wandered off. I'm sure if you leave them alone, they'll come home."

"You don't understand. They've never wandered off before. I think someone stole my sheep!" She tugged on her bonnet strings with trembling fingers.

"Well, I'll file a report, but I'm betting they'll be back by nightfall. In the meantime, we'll keep our eyes open for them." He slid his notebook into his front shirt pocket and tipped his hat to her. "Good day to you, Miss Peep."

"Good day to you, Officer Wolfe." Little Bo Peep inclined her head.

She stood watching his taillights fade into the distance with narrowed eyes. She pulled her cell phone out of her pocket and dialed.

"Hello, Red. I need your help. My sheep are gone." Little Bo Peep clutched her phone.

"I'll be right there," Little Red Riding Hood's voice echoed through the bad connection.

Little Bo Peep was searching the meadow for clues when Little Red Riding Hood arrived in her bright red Jeep.

"Oh, Bo, I'm so sorry you lost your sheep! When did they disappear? Any idea where to find them?" Little Red Riding Hood ran up to Little Bo Peep and hugged her.

"No. I can't tell where to find them. They disappeared while we were having lunch. I found some tire tracks over here. They lead into the hills. Do you think we could follow them in your Jeep?"

Little Red Riding Hood laughed. "My Jeep can go anywhere! Let's go find your missing sheep."

They climbed into the car and picked their way through the hills until the path turned to paving stone.

"Let's go talk to some people and see if anyone saw my sheep," Little Bo Peep suggested.

"That's a good idea. The old woman who lives in a shoe with all her kids isn't far from here. Let's start with her."

They drove down the paved lane to the giant shoe that had been converted into a house. They managed to get into the driveway without running over any children, but they were overwhelmed by little voices as soon as they stepped out of the Jeep.

"Can you tell me where to find your mommy?" Little Bo Peep asked one of the boys.

"In the back yard," he replied before skipping off.

They ventured into the back yard and found the old mother washing windows with a child wrapped around each of her legs.

"Excuse us," Little Bo Peep said, "I've lost my sheep and can't tell where to find them. Have you seen a dozen sheep with pink ear tags?"

The old woman brushed her gray hair out of her eyes and regarded her two visitors. "No. If they'd come this way, my kids would be riding around on them right now. You might check with the little boy who lives down the lane, though. He has a sheep. Maybe yours went to visit his." She shrugged and resumed cleaning her windows.

Little Red Riding Hood and Little Bo Peep climbed back in the Jeep and went in search of the little boy who lives down the lane. They found him pacing up and down the road.

"Baa Baa! Baa Baa Black Sheep, where are you?" he cried.

"Have you lost your sheep, too?" Little Bo Peep asked.

"Yes. Baa Baa Black Sheep left with two bags of wool this morning. He left one bag of wool at my house, and he was supposed to take the other two to the master and the dame, but he never arrived. Where could he have gone?"

"My sheep went missing this morning, too. I had lunch with Little Red Riding Hood, and they were gone when I returned to the meadow. I suspect they were sheepnapped!"

"Oh no! I bet whoever took your sheep took Baa Baa, too. We have to find them! Baa Baa was just shorn, and he'll be so cold tonight." He shuffled his feet.

"Come with us. We're questioning everyone. We're sure to find them," Little Red Riding Hood said.

They all climbed in the Jeep and took off down the lane. They pulled into Old Mother Hubbard's driveway where they were met by her skinny dog.

"The poor thing looks hungry," Little Red Riding Hood said.

She walked to the back of her Jeep and opened the rear door. She reached into her basket of goodies and removed a peanut butter sandwich. She held it out to the poor pooch who gobbled it up. She hooked the basket over her arm and marched up to the door.

Old Mother Hubbard answered the door with a sad smile. "Oh my, I wasn't expecting visitors. I'm afraid my cupboards are bare, so I have no refreshments to share."

Little Red Riding Hood held out her basket of goodies. "We've brought the refreshments today. We'd like to ask you some questions while we enjoy them if we may."

"Oh, how delightful! Yes, please come in," she said stepping aside.

After everyone was seated comfortably at the kitchen table and had eaten sandwiches and cookies, Little Bo Peep regarded the old woman.

"Have you seen any sheep around here? We're missing a dozen white sheep with pink ear tags and one freshly shorn black sheep."

"I haven't seen them, but I heard a commotion late this morning. I was searching for berries in the woods when I heard some sheep bleating. The noise was coming from the direction of Little Boy Blue's place." She helped herself to another cookie.

"Thank you, Old Mother Hubbard. We appreciate your help. Please keep the basket of goodies to share with your dog," Little Red Riding Hood said standing.

The three sheep searchers hurried to the Jeep and made their way to Little Boy Blue's farm. He was nowhere to be found, but his cows were in the corn patch having a heyday.

"What in the world?" Little Bo Peep cried. She clapped and hollered at the cows, but they wouldn't budge. "We need to find Little Boy Blue. Those cows only respond to his horn."

They searched the house and the barn. "Little Boy Blue, where are you?" they hollered.

Little Red Riding Hood made her way to the meadow and froze in her tracks.

"Come quick!" She motioned them forward. "I've found them!"

They ran to the meadow and found their sheep grazing with several others.

"There are my sheep and Baa Baa Black

Sheep." Little Bo Peep sagged in relief. She pointed to a tiny lamb. "Is that Mary's little lamb that followed her to school one day?"

"Yes, I think it is. She's still in class, so she wouldn't know her little lamb is missing. We need to find Little Boy Blue and get to the bottom of this," Little Red Riding Hood said. "I'm calling the police."

Little Bo Peep found him sleeping under a hay cart. She stomped over to him and yanked on his ear. "Little Boy Blue, wake up! You have sheep that don't belong to you in the meadow, and your cows are in the corn. Wake up!"

Little Boy Blue sat up and rubbed his eyes. He glared at Little Bo Peep. "I know where my cows are. I don't have to pick the corn this way."

Officer Wolfe arrived and joined them just as Little Red Riding Hood confronted the sheep thief.

"Explain why you have rustled sheep in your meadow," she demanded.

Officer Wolfe folded his arms across his chest. "Yes, please explain that to us."

Little Boy Blue looked at him with big blue puppy dog eyes. "I owe the Farmer in the Dell some money. He agreed to accept sheep instead of cash, but I didn't have enough. I had to get more. But now everyone can have their sheep back. No harm done. Right?"

"I'm afraid not. You're under arrest for sheep rustling." Officer Wolfe handcuffed Little Boy Blue and led him to his car.

"Now that's solved, but how are we going to get all of these sheep back to their homes?" Little Bo Peep asked.

"No problem," Little Red Riding Hood said. "We'll hook Little Boy Blue's trailer up to my Jeep and have them home in no time."

The sheep were all home by nightfall, wagging their tails behind them.

ASHES IN THE EVENING

Home alone trying to figure out what to do with my life, I heard a knock on my door. A little boy smiled up at me when I peered out the window. He looked like an angel with bright blue eyes and flowing golden hair, framing his face like a halo. He looked a little too perfect, his smile just a little too practiced for my comfort. If he hadn't already seen me through the window, I probably would have ignored him and gone back to my brooding. Instead, I opened the door with the expectation that he was selling something.

"Hello. I'm Johnny." He grinned up at me. "I'm selling candles for a school fundraiser. Would it be all right for me to come in and show you the catalog?"

I'd always bought that kind of thing from my step-children, and I still had plenty. I was about to turn him away when I found myself saying, "Yes, please come in and show me your catalog."

He waltzed into my home like he owned the place while I was still trying to figure out why I'd invited this kid inside. I felt the fine hairs on the back of my neck stand on end as he walked into the living room and looked around with a great deal of interest.

"So, Johnny, where's your catalog?" I asked.

"Do you live here alone?" His eyes took on a reddish glow.

"Yes," I replied. "I'm recently divorced and never had children."

"What is your name?"

"Stephanie." *Why am I having this conversation? Why can't I control my own body or the words I speak?*

"I am going to stay with you for a while, Stephanie. I am your nephew from out of town who needs a place to stay."

I heard myself say, "Yes, Johnny. You are my nephew from out of town. You will be staying with me for a while."

His smile was one of pure evil. "Yes, that's a good girl. By tomorrow you will believe that with all of your heart."

My entire body felt like it was mired in swamp mud, but I gathered enough strength to ask, "What do you want from me, Johnny?"

He explored my living room and kept me waiting for an answer. He slid his fingers over the TV, touched knickknacks here and there, and examined the photos on my mantle before turning back to me with a response.

"I need a home for now. I require a safe place to sleep and a living blood source."

My stomach twisted and my heart raced. "Blood source?"

"I am a vampire, Aunt Stephanie." He spoke the words as casually as if he were telling me about his favorite color.

Vampire? Did he say he's a vampire? I must be dreaming! Vampires are mythological. There's no way he's a vampire. I must've fallen and hit my head on something. That's why I can't control my body. I'm dreaming.

Johnny must've sensed my thoughts

because he bared his fangs at me and hissed. "Yes, I am a vampire. Never doubt my word. My word is now your world."

All of my life's regrets rushed back to me. My marriage ended, and my parents had both passed on from this world. I'd moved hundreds of miles from my friends. I never had children of my own because I let my ex-husband convince me that his were enough. They never bothered to visit or extend an invitation for me to visit.

Left with the ashes of my life, I'd moved to a city where I knew no one. I'd wanted a fresh, clean start. I didn't even have a job yet, still living on my half of the proceeds from the sale of our house. I was this vampire's perfect choice of victim. No one would ever miss me.

Johnny didn't look like a vampire. He looked like an innocent ten-year old boy who spent his spare time playing video games. I had a feeling that his wholesome good looks were his secret weapon and wondered how many other unsuspecting women he'd victimized.

"Don't look so sad, Aunt Stephanie," he said. "I'm not going to hurt you if you're good and do what I tell you. I'm going to stay here where you can protect me during the day and entertain me at night."

"Why do you need my protection if you're a vampire? Don't you have super strength and preternatural speed? How do you expect me to protect you any better than you can protect yourself?"

His lips flattened in irritation. "I'm being hunted. I only require protection during the day. I can take care of myself at night when I am awake. I'm staying here, and you'll protect me with your life while I rest. I control you and everything you do from now on. Don't lie and tell me that you have to leave the house for work. I've been watching you, and I know your routine. The only person who ever comes to visit you is the Avon lady."

"Do your eyes always glow when you're angry? How are you controlling me? I still have a will of my own, but it's like I'm your puppet. Why did you choose me? Who's hunting you? What makes you think I won't just leave when you go to sleep?" I couldn't stop the questions that flew from my lips like a swarm of bees.

"Aunt Stephanie, you need to feed me. We can talk more after I've eaten. Perhaps

I'll feel generous enough to answer your questions then. Be certain of one thing; from this point forward, I'm in control of everything you do. Now hold still."

I couldn't move at all, even though everything inside me screamed for me to run. Johnny approached me wearing that evil smile I already hated. He lifted my wrist to his mouth and inhaled deeply like he was scenting fine wine. A burning pain the likes of which I've never known hit me when he bit into my wrist. I cried out in agony, and then couldn't utter another peep.

I stood helpless to do anything but stare at Johnny's fangs puncturing my wrist and the tiny drop of my blood caught in the corner of his mouth. He continued taking long pulls from my wrist like a human child would a milkshake. The pain traveled from my wrist up my arm to my shoulder. My wrist was red where my blood rushed to the surface, but the rest of my arm was ghostly white. I didn't know how much more I could endure. I was getting dizzy and felt unconsciousness approaching.

What am I going to do? Is he going to kill me when he's finished with me? Will he make me into a vampire like him? Is there any escape? Do I have anything I can use as a weapon? What would even hurt a vampire? How long will it be before someone notices I'm gone?

Johnny finally had his fill of my blood and retracted his fangs. He licked my wrist and then his lips with a satisfied smile. Pulling a large bandage from his pocket, he opened it and applied it to my wrist. His cheeks were rosy, his lips crimson.

He opened his mouth to speak, but was cut off by the crash of a window breaking behind me. It took me a moment to realize that I'd regained control of my body. I stumbled toward the front door, but Johnny cut me off and threw me to the floor behind the couch.

"Stay down or you could get caught in the middle of this, and it's going to be ugly. There's usually more than one of them. I still have plans for you, and they require you to be alive." The red glow of his evil eyes made my heart thunder in my chest.

I peeked over the couch and saw a giant man squaring off with Johnny. He had a loaded crossbow in his hand, bolts in a quiver on his back, and several wooden stakes stuffed into the pockets of his camouflage fatigues. I was about to warn him that Johnny was more dangerous than he looked when they started taunting each other.

"I am two thousand years old. I was born a prince. It will take more than a common mutt like you to end me. My royal blood always wins!" Johnny sneered.

The hulking man was well over six feet tall and had a muscular physique straight off a body building magazine. His army green T-shirt stretched over his chest and around his enormous arms. With dark brown hair was cut close to his scalp in a military style, he was a handsome warrior who would have had me blushing under any other circumstances. Where Johnny looked like an innocent angel, this man looked like he'd danced with the devil a few times.

His nut-brown eyes burned with anger and hatred as he snarled back at Johnny, "I've hunted you for over twenty years, and today you'll pay for wiping out my pack!"

"Ah, the lone wolf is here to have his revenge. How very last century of you," Johnny laughed.

This standoff would've been comical if I'd seen it on TV. The warrior looked like he was about to eat the little boy for breakfast, but I knew what that boy really was. My hands trembled with fear as I watched the confrontation take place in my living room just a few feet from me. The man lifted his crossbow and fired so quickly that I could barely follow his movements.

Johnny moved too fast for me to see, and the bolt hit the floor where he'd been standing. One second he was standing in the middle of the room and the next he'd leapt onto the man's back and had his fangs stuck in the warrior's throat.

The man somehow managed to shake Johnny loose and send him flying across the room. He'd dropped his crossbow in the tussle, so he grabbed a stake from his pocket and lunged for the vampire. Johnny proved too quick for the man again and punched him in the stomach. The warrior crashed into the wall. I cringed at the crunch of his bolt quiver being crushed between the wall and his body.

As I watched, the man's body started changing shape, and his clothes dropped off of him in tatters. I heard several revolting pops and cracks before a huge brown wolf stood where the man had just been.

This cannot be real. Vampires and werewolves are not real.

I was shocked to see that Johnny changed, too. His angelic blond hair and blue eyes were replaced with stringy dark hair that hung to his shoulders in limp hunks. His eyes looked like two burning coals. His cheeks were sunken in. He grew taller, and his limbs grew longer with massive claws tipping each finger and toe. His skin turned the gray of death and every muscle was defined in sickening detail.

The two monsters were more evenly matched now. They were a blur of motion rolling around together on the floor punching, kicking, biting, and scratching each other.

Keeping a close eye on them, I crept across the room to where the wolf man's clothes lay in a shredded pile. I dug around in the pile until I found a couple of stakes. The monsters might be between the door and me, but I was nobody's damsel in distress. I refused to face the winner of this fight without a weapon. The crossbow would be preferable, but I couldn't find it.

The creatures broke apart looking exhausted. The wolf swayed with the effort to stand and changed back into a man. Bleeding from dozens of cuts, bites, and scratches, he leaned against the far wall and looked too exhausted to move.

Johnny was moving slower than before, also sporting several cuts, scratches, and bites. His eyes weren't glowing anymore and had a weary look about them. However, his wounds were healing quicker than the wolf man's. I could only guess that was because he'd so recently partaken of my blood.

I tried to be as still as possible, so I wouldn't draw either monster's attention, certain that my survival depended on remaining unnoticed.

As I watched, Johnny's lips curled into a triumphant smile. He reached behind a chair and lifted the crossbow. He had the weapon, but the bolts for it were in the pile of clothes where I was crouched.

"Aunt Stephanie, bring those bolts to me now." Johnny's voice was rough and guttural.

I could feel my body being compelled to do his bidding, but I was still in control. His power over me must've weakened in the fight. I hadn't been able to resist him the other times he'd forced his will on me.

Stalling for time, I slowly reached into the clothing and moved it around pretending to look for the bolts.

"No, don't do it," the wolf man begged me softly. "He'll kill you once you've served your purpose. He's a liar, manipulator, and murderer. He's the very definition of evil."

"I can't find them." I shot the wolf man a quick glance from beneath my lashes before looking up at Johnny. "They must've been thrown under the furniture or something when he changed form."

"You are worthless." Johnny stomped over to where I crouched. "Perhaps I should rethink our arrangement."

When he knelt next to me to rummage through the pile, I knew in my heart what I needed to do in order to survive. I only had one chance. He'd kill me if I failed.

Johnny still believed he had control of me. Overconfidence made him sloppy. Before I could change my mind, I grabbed the two stakes I'd found earlier and plunged one of them into his chest as hard and fast as I could. He screeched and backhanded me across the face. I fell back and smacked my head on the wall hard enough to see stars.

Trying to dislodge the stake, he didn't see the wolf man coming up behind him. With no time to think, I just acted, and tossed the stake I still clutched to the wolf man. He plunged it into Johnny's back hard enough to pierce the vampire's heart. Johnny exploded into ashes, which covered my living room, the wolf man, and me.

The two of us stared at each other for a long moment trying to process what happened. "Are you okay? You're covered in vampire ash." He studied me with a concerned frown.

I nodded. "Are you okay? You're covered in blood and vampire ash."

"I'll be fine." He gave me a crooked smile.

"Will I become a vampire? He bit me." I couldn't keep the tremor from my voice.

"No. He would've had to drain all of your blood and then give you some of his in order for you to become a vampire. You'll be weak for a while, but you'll be fine."

"Who are you?" I asked.

"My name is Gabriel. I've been hunting that filthy little vampire for years. I came close to him several times, but he always got away. He murdered my entire community. He killed everyone including the children. Thanks to you, he'll never kill again. I owe you my life and my gratitude. My honor is restored." He inclined his head to me.

"He mentioned he was some sort of prince. Does that mean he was a royal vampire? Like the son of the vampire king or something?" I asked.

"I've done much research into his past in my quest for justice and know the entire story. Johnny was born a human prince thousands of years ago. His parents angered a master vampire when they demanded tribute from him. The vampire marched into the court one evening, grabbed Johnny by the hair, and turned him in front of his parents. He wanted the king and queen to know their precious heir would never become the mighty king they'd hoped. Then while Johnny watched helplessly from the throne room floor, the master killed the monarchs."

"That's horrible," I whispered.

"He left Johnny there to fend for himself, which is why he's always been a lone vampire. No master would claim him." Gabriel sighed. "Have no pity for that monster, though. He was a sadistic child and has always been the most vicious of vampires."

"Yes, I got that impression. Don't worry, I could never pity him." I finally noticed Gabriel was standing in my living room naked and bleeding while I peppered him with questions.

"Can I get you some bandages and maybe a sheet to cover up with?" I watched a trickle of blood make its way down his massive chest.

"Thank you, but no. I must go now to heal as nature intended. I'll return in the morning to help you clean up. Johnny worked alone, so you should be okay for now. But, he wasn't the only monster who prowls the night. I won't be far away, and I'll be here at the first sign of trouble, sweet Stephanie."

Gabriel returned to his wolf form and leapt out the same window he'd used to enter my house. Alone again with a wicked mess to clean up and enough potential nightmares to last a lifetime, I wondered how Gabriel would know if I ever needed him. I shuddered when I pictured the kind of trouble that would bring him back to my house.

Two mythological creatures entered my home that evening. One was evil while the other was honorable. I'd been helpless against them and could've died.

I noticed the crossbow on the floor and hefted it onto my shoulder. I would be prepared if another monster ever knocked on my door. Smiling, I rose from the ashes.

RUNAWAY ASSES

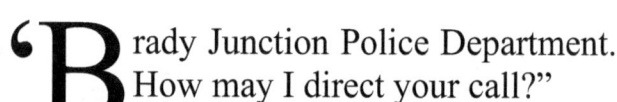

"Brady Junction Police Department. How may I direct your call?"

"I'm not sure. I don't know who to call." I stated my name and address before blurting, "I have four donkeys in my back yard, and they're driving my dog crazy."

"Just to confirm, you said you have four donkeys in your back yard. Is that correct?"

"Yes, that's correct. I don't know what to do about it. I realize this is a small town, but I never thought I'd have livestock grazing in my backyard."

"I will send an officer over to take care of the issue."

I hung up the phone feeling foolish. Who

in the world has stray donkeys show up in the middle of town? I looked down at my little black and white Chihuahua who hadn't stopped barking since he discovered the interlopers in his territory.

"Hush, Hermes. We should be rid of the donkeys soon." I scooped him up in my arms. He trembled violently in agitation before finally quieting down.

My doorbell rang a few minutes later, and the barking began again. I answered the door to a tall police officer with dark brown hair and the bluest eyes I'd ever seen. He was built like a fighter with a broad chest and bulging biceps that strained his blue uniform shirt. I couldn't help but stare for a moment.

"Abigail Stewart? I'm Officer Martin. I understand you're having some animal issues."

"Yes, there are four donkeys in my back yard, and Hermes here is having a fit," I replied.

"Let's see what we're dealing with," Officer Martin said heading toward the back yard.

His brisk walk held a hint of swagger. I could tell this man was confident in his abilities. I couldn't help but smile as I imagined him wrangling the errant donkeys.

"HEEHAW!"

Officer Martin stopped abruptly at the sound and drew his weapon.

"That was a donkey braying," I said over Hermes' renewed barking.

"222," the police radio crackled.

"222," answered Officer Martin.

"Be advised, we have found the owner of the donkeys. He's on his way to your location."

"Copy," Officer Martin replied.

He turned to me with a smile "We just need to keep them corralled until the owner gets here. Have you noticed any damage?"

I pointed to one of the donkeys cheerfully munching on vegetables in the middle of my garden. My once lush plants were trampled beyond recognition. While I was distracted, Hermes leapt out of my grasp and raced toward the veggie thief barking and snarling. The donkey looked at him, lowered his head, and lumbered toward him.

"Oh, no!" I screamed and ran toward the doggie versus donkey standoff.

"Wait!" cried Officer Martin. "You could injure yourself!"

I wasn't listening. Rescuing Hermes was

my sole focus. I slid to a stop between the two animals, mere inches from the donkey. I scooped up Hermes and spun on my heel to run away. My foot slipped in the grass, and I fell flat on my butt. I looked up in horror as the donkey closed in on me. My tumble had only increased Hermes' snarling and growling.

The donkey looked at me and said, "HEEHAW!"

"Don-key! Don-key! Here, Don-key!" Officer Martin shouted, waving his arms.

He successfully distracted the donkey long enough for me to get to my feet and run back to the house. I opened the back door and shoved Hermes inside. Looking back, I saw the other three donkeys ambling closer to the officer. I didn't know anything about donkeys, but they were large animals and sure looked like they could hurt one lone guy.

I dashed into the house and grabbed a bag of carrots from the fridge. Then I ran back outside waving a carrot around like I was wielding a mighty sword.

"Donkeys!" I shouted waving my orange veggie sword. "I have carrots! Come get them!"

I tossed one carrot after another to the corner of my yard. The donkeys noticed and meandered over to nibble. I sagged in relief as the aggressive donkey joined the other three for the free carrot feast.

"What were you thinking?" Officer Martin asked coming up beside me.

"I was thinking those donkeys look pretty stout. I sure didn't want to watch you get your butt kicked by a few runaway asses."

He stared at me for a moment and then laughed long and loud. He continued to laugh so hard that he could hardly stand up. Then I started laughing. The entire episode had been surreal. Our laughter finally subsided when the farmer arrived to collect his donkeys.

The runaways seemed happy enough to file into the trailer, and the farmer was beyond apologetic. "I'm so sorry," he said. "They've never gotten out before. At least they stayed together. They traveled two miles to get here. Did they damage anything?"

"Just my garden and nerves," I replied shaking my head. I pointed to the veggie thief and said, "That ass had a heyday destroying my cabbage."

He looked over at my garden and winced. "I'm so sorry. I'll pay for the damage."

"No need," I said shaking my head. "Just keep your asses corralled, and I'll be happy."

"You know, asses are wild, and donkeys are the domesticated descendants of asses. They're called burrows in Mexico." Something about my facial expression made him stop before he shared any more trivia.

"Have a nice evening!" The farmer waved as he hopped in his truck and drove away.

Officer Martin cleared the call and turned to me. "Well, you were my last call of the evening. I'm officially off work now," he said with a smile.

"Have you eaten dinner, Officer?" I twirled a lock of hair around my finger.

"No, I haven't." I swear his eyes actually twinkled.

"All of this action made me really hungry. Would you like to join me for some pizza?"

"Yes, I'd love to join you. I just need to go back to the station, drop off my car, and change clothes. I can be back here in half an hour. Is that good for you?" he asked.

"Yeah, that's good for me, Officer," I answered with a grin.

"Call me Seth." His smile held a promise. "After herding asses together, I think we're beyond formalities."

"You're absolutely right. Please call me Abby."

I glanced in the hall mirror after Seth left and gasped at what I saw. My long brown hair was in rats. There was mud streaked across my fair cheek, and my brown eyes had smudges of who knew what beneath them. I looked down at my muddy jeans, and ran to the bathroom. I took the fastest shower of my life, dried and tamed my hair, dressed in clean jeans with a purple peasant top, and even slapped on some light makeup before he returned.

Seth rang my doorbell, and I breathed deeply to find my inner calm. I opened the door with a smile. He wore a dark T-shirt and faded jeans that hugged his powerful thighs.

He grinned when he saw I'd cleaned up for him. "Shall we go?"

"Yes, I'm ready." I fought to keep my breathing steady.

He helped me into his old Chevy truck and drove us to the only pizza place in our small town. We ordered a large chicken bacon ranch pizza and then stared at each other. The silence stretched on until I couldn't take it anymore.

"So, was this your first time with a donkey disturbance?" I asked.

He laughed. The sound was rich and smoky, reminding me of a fine whiskey. "Yeah, most animal calls involve stray dogs. Once in a while I have to deal with a raccoon, but that was my first donkey call."

"Well, I think you handled it very well for your first time." I gave him my best flirty smile.

His good-natured smile faded away. "Why did you run out between two aggressive animals like that? You could have been seriously hurt."

My playfulness fled. "Hermes means the world to me. I wasn't about to let him get hurt. I realize that he has an alligator mouth and a hummingbird butt, but he's my sweet baby."

"Next time, let me deal with that stuff. I'd hate for something bad to happen to you."

"Next time? You say that like you plan to be around for a next time."

His lips lifted into a sexy grin. "It's not every day I meet a woman who runs at an angry donkey to save a little dog. I'd like to get to know you better."

"I'd like that, too," I said softly just as our pizza arrived.

After a pleasant dinner, Seth drove me home and walked me to my door like a true gentleman. "Would you like to come in for some coffee or tea?"

"I better not tonight. I have an early shift tomorrow. I'd really like to see you again, though. Are you free Saturday night?"

"Yes, I'm free, and I'd love to see you!" My reply was a little too eager.

He chuckled and lifted a hand to brush a lock of my hair behind my ear. He lowered his head ever so slowly, building the anticipation until I thought I would explode. Finally, his lips caressed mine like warm sunshine on a tranquil lake. When we broke apart, we stared into each other's eyes for a long time.

"I'll see you Saturday, Mighty Ass Slayer."

I watched him saunter away, and I couldn't help but ponder strange quirks of fate. We would never have met if it hadn't been for some bored donkeys that wanted to be bad asses.

ABOUT THE AUTHOR

Margarite Stever grew up in Asbury, a tiny Missouri town of just over 200 people. She has a Bachelor of Arts Degree in English from Missouri Southern State University. She writes stories and essays that touch a person's heart.

Stever is a member of Joplin Writers' Guild, Missouri Writers Guild, Sleuths' Ink Mystery Writers, Ozarks Writers League, and Ozarks Romance Authors. Her work has recently appeared in *Chicken Soup for the Soul: It's Beginning to Look a Lot Like Christmas;* Joplin Writers' Guild Anthology, *Seasons of the Four States; Anthology 2019 Sleuths' Ink Mystery Writers*; *Missouri's Emerging Writers*; *Legends: Passion Pages*; *50-Word Stories* website; the 2021, 2019, 2018, 2017, and 2016 issues of *The Crowder Quill;* the Fall 2015 issue of *The Maine Review; Mamalode Magazine's 2015 Better Together;* and *Writer's Digest 2014 Show Us Your Shorts Collection.*

Her seeds of wisdom and joy can be read at ozarksmaven.com, which has been read in over 80 countries.